A BADGER TALE

A BADGER TALE

Adventures of a Wisconsin Farm Family

JAMES R. VYVYAN SR.

To order additional copies of this book, contact:
Xlibris
1-888-795-4274
www.Xlibris.com
Orders@Xlibris.com
717726

CONTENTS

Book Three: John Foxwell

ACKNOWLEDGMENTS

Technical Advisor: Richard Reul
Editors: Erin Lingsweiler and Megan Meneau
Additional thanks to Barbara Felix and Arliss Reul.

Dum vivimus vivamus and *sapere aude.*

PROLOGUE

YESTERDAY WAS THE best day of my life. I, John Foxwell, had the grand champion steer, won the pulling contest with my dad's Allis Chalmers tractor, and word got back to me that the prettiest girl in Yorkville likes me. Life is good! (I didn't know it then, but it would be a long time before I felt this way again.)

It was 6:00 a.m., and the sun was rising, and it was time to help my dad, Tom Foxwell Jr., with the milking. Yet something didn't feel right; maybe it was just me coming down to earth after yesterday's excitement. As I was walking toward the barn, the sky was growing darker, and there were storm clouds on the horizon.

"Hi, Dad, sure looks like we've got some ugly weather heading our way." Dad nodded. I turned on the radio. Except for the market reports, Dad hated the radio and what he called the newfangled music. I, on the other hand, couldn't wait to hear my favorite song, "Please Send Me Someone to Love" by Percy Mayfield. That was not to be. What we heard was a news flash—President Truman had sent troops into North Korea. Holy shit, I was only two years away from being eligible for the draft!

We milked the twenty-nine cows in silence. Dad wasn't much of a talker, at least not with me. The only sound was the rhythmic *click, click* of the milking machines. As we finished milking, I thought, where was my dog Blackie? I had raised Blackie from a pup, and for the last ten years, he was the first to greet me as I walked to the barn. I left the barn and took a quick right to his doghouse. As I approached, I saw a trail of blood. Blackie lay dead at the door to his house; someone or something had ripped open his stomach. Through my tears, it dawned on me that last year the same thing happened to our best calf.

BOOK ONE

Tom Foxwell Sr.

CHAPTER ONE

Birthdays

A S USUAL, WE were sitting in the last pew of the Yorkville Methodist Church. We always sat in the last pew because the morning farm chores always seemed to run late, and we would try to sneak into church without being seen. There we were, Ma; Pa; older brothers, Walter and Ben; sister, Mame; and me. I had had two more brothers, but they died last year after getting a terrible cough from which they never recovered. The preacher, Reverend Hollowell, was droning on about the sins of drinking, gambling, and dancing. I, on the other hand, was thinking happy thoughts; today was my birthday. We kind of celebrated last night; Ma and Pa gave me my first watch for my sixteenth birthday. Walter gave me a pack of Wrigley's chewing gum, which is my absolute favorite treat. (I'll never forget a few years ago when Ma bought a can of baking powder and a pack of gum was attached. Wrigley no longer gives the gum away for free; in fact, I don't think they even make baking powder anymore.) Ben promised me a fireworks display for my birthday. (I hoped it would be at least as good as what he did for last New Year's Eve when we entered the new century.) Sister Mame was just a year older than me and was really the only sibling I could talk to. I'm sure she feels the same about me. We share secrets and help each other out when trouble is brewing. Mame made me a quilt for my birthday. I don't know how she did it. It must have taken over a hundred hours to make, yet I never saw her working on it. Mame is really something; she can do anything she sets her mind to.

You might wonder why we celebrated my birthday last night. The answer is the real reason I'm thinking happy thoughts. I've been invited to a party! I'll try to explain. I went to Yorkville School for eight years. Yorkville School is a one-room school with grades one through eight taught by a single teacher. By *single* I mean there was only one teacher, and that teacher had to be single. Married women were not allowed to teach at Yorkville. There were only three students in my grade: Linda Shunk, Joe Maranger, and me. I was always sweet on Linda but too shy to say it or show it. Even last year, a year after we graduated, Linda came up to me at the Racine County Fair and said, "Hi, Tom, how are you?"

I replied, "Ah, ah, ah, I gotta go," and ran off. How could I be so stupid? Even remembering it makes me furious with myself!

Where am I going with this? Oh yeah, the party. After graduation, Linda went on to the brand-new high school in Union Grove. I, on the other hand, was needed on the farm. So for the last two years, I've only seen Linda three times, including that time at the fair. Then, out of the blue, an invitation came to attend her birthday party. Did I mention that she and I had the same birthday? I've been told that on the day we were born, Doc Moyle almost drove himself crazy driving his buggy back and forth the three miles between our house and the Shunks.

Although I was excited and happy about the invitation, that soon transformed into a kind of terror. I would have to get a present! I didn't have a lot of money, but even if I did, a present that was too expensive would show too much of how I felt. A present that was too cheap wouldn't send the message that I was sweet on her. What to do, what to do? One day, Ma asked me to get some ice for our icebox. So I took our team of horses—George and Abraham, named after the presidents—to get some ice from Vivian's ice house. The Yorkville store was right next door, so I walked over, and as I entered, Mr. McQuarry said, "Hi, Tom, what ya looking fer?"

I said, "Nothing—just lookin'." I looked and looked, but I knew if I took too long, my brothers would get wind of it and tease the daylights out of me. Finally, I saw some stationery that had some blue violets painted in the four corners, so I said, "Mr. McQuarry, how much for this paper?"

"Ten cents."

"I'll take it."

For the next week, I worried. Was the gift too much or too little? Finally, I decided it might be too little to show Linda how I felt. So I asked Mame, "Could you do some of that fancy writing for me?"

Mame said quietly, "It's called calligraphy, Tom."

"I was wondering if you would write 'Linda' at the top of each of these ten sheets, and don't you dare tell Pa or our brothers."

Mame replied, "It'll be our little secret."

JAMES R. VYVYAN SR.

I'd dressed extra carefully this morning since I was leaving for the party right after church. I had on my best white cotton shirt and black wool pants with black suspenders. The pants were a little long since they once belonged to my brother Ben. (Ma assured me that I would soon grow into them.) I also wore my new black leather shoes with pointed toes. Those shoes hurt like the dickens, and my toes were piled one on top of the other, but when Ma and I went to the Yorkville General Store to buy them, I told her they felt great. I just wanted to wear shoes like the ones that I had seen in *LIFE* magazine.

After church, I mounted my horse Toby. I liked to think of Toby as the fastest horse in Yorkville, and I was very proud of her. The three-mile journey to Linda's house gave me a lot of time to think. Did she invite just me? If she did, that would be great. Or would it? If it was just me, I'd have to make conversation all afternoon. Did she invite the whole neighborhood? Then I wouldn't have to make much conversation, but it wouldn't make me feel special either. Did she feel about me the way I felt about her? For a shy person like me, time to think was not always a good thing. By the time I got to Linda's house, my heart was pounding.

As I tied Toby to the fence, I spotted Linda, Joe Maranger, and a girl, who turned out to be Linda's cousin Patricia, sticking small metal hoops into the ground. I managed to get out a quiet "Happy birthday, what ya doin'?"

"We're setting up to play croquet, silly."

I'd never heard of croquet, and I thought, *I hope I don't make a fool of myself playing this silly game.* As I looked around, I saw a total of twelve people, all about my age. Of course I knew Linda and Joe; all the rest were strangers to me. It turned out they all went to St. Mary's Catholic church like Linda did.

I took time to look at Linda. Linda had beautiful blond hair tied back with a dark blue ribbon and flowing down the back of her neck. She had on a light blue cotton dress with a tiny bow at the neck. The dress fell a little below her knees with dark blue stocking so that virtually no skin showed unless she moved quickly or the wind blew. She too had pointed black leather shoes; I hoped for her sake they caused less pain than mine. The blue in her ribbon, dress, and stockings all seemed to highlight the blue in her eyes. In short, she was beautiful.

We all gathered under the big oak tree in her backyard, where we had lemonade and egg salad sandwiches, followed by apple pie with homemade ice cream. I managed to get out a few words with Joe but was really too shy to talk to any of the other partygoers. Then Linda announced that it was time for croquet. There were to be three groups of four, and the winners would play each other for the championship. Soon it was my turn to hit the ball. How hard do you hit a croquet ball? I didn't want to appear to be a wimp. I thought to myself, *Erring on the side of hitting it too hard would be better than hitting it too weakly.* So I pulled the mallet back, and the moment I struck the ball, I thought, *Oh shit.* The ball traveled across the yard and into the Skeweses' cornfield. It must have traveled 150 feet! I wished I could have crawled into a hole. Needless to say, I was soon eliminated and watched quietly as the game continued with Joe Maranger being the eventual winner.

Then Linda announced we would have a treasure hunt. That sounded like fun; I've had treasure hunts before, and I thought, *I've got this handled.* Then Linda added, "All the clues will be in pig Latin."

Several people shouted, "What the heck is pig Latin?"

Linda replied, "Surely you've heard of pig Latin! Even President Jefferson wrote some of his notes in pig Latin. Anyway, only the captain of each team needs to be able to read pig Latin. So raise your hand if you can read pig Latin."

I raised my hand and then immediately thought, *Why did I do that?* I've never even heard of pig Latin until today. So there I was, captain of our team of four, and I had to decipher the clues. Needless to say, we didn't win.

We then gathered under the oak tree for the opening of the presents. I won't bore you with all the presents; I'll just skip to mine. She opened it slowly and, as far as I could tell, really liked it because she looked me right in my eyes and said, "Thank you, I've never seen anything so beautiful!" I was in heaven. However, heaven didn't seem to last very long for me, and shortly, I was feeling shy and uncomfortable again. So I said my least favorite words, "Ah . . . ah . . . I gotta go, time to milk the cows."

I slowly walked toward Toby, but just as I got there, Linda was by my side. "You didn't think I'd forgotten about your birthday, did you?" As usual, I was speechless.

"I have something for you." She handed me a roll of paper tied with a blue ribbon.

JAMES R. VYVYAN SR.

I quickly opened it, and it was a picture she had drawn showing a horse with a young man standing by the horse. Wait a minute, it's not just any horse—that's Toby, and son of a gun—that's me! I reached for her hand and said, "I love it, and I'll never forget this—thank you!" In the back of my head, I thought, *I actually touched a girl on purpose! Wow!* Plus I had said something that actually made sense. Maybe I was making progress.

On the first mile of the trip home, I kept thinking, *She likes me . . . she likes me . . . she likes me.* On the second mile home, I kept thinking, *When will I ever see her again? I can't wait until her next birthday!* On the third mile, I thought, *She'll be going back to high school this fall, and she'll fall in love with one of the football players.* Why does life have to be so hard? Does everybody torture themselves the way I do?

CHAPTER TWO

Harvest Time

THE LAST FEW days have been rough. Harvest time is never easy, but this year was extraordinary. Let me give you some background before I get to the details.

The old timers talk about the days when they would lay their oats or wheat on a hard surface and pound the grain with some sort of stick to separate the grain from the straw and chaff. On a good day, they might be able to get about ten to twenty bushels of grain.

Today, we harvest with a threshing machine, powered by a steam engine. We can harvest up to one thousand bushels of grain in a day! However, the threshing machine and steam engine cost about $1,500! You may not realize it, but presently you can buy a small farm for $1,500! Plus, it takes ten to fifteen men to operate these machines. Therefore, no farmer has the help or the money to own one of these machines, without some sort of cooperation with his neighbors.

We are lucky in one regard because the Threshing Machine King lives and builds these machines just fifteen miles east in Racine, Wisconsin. The Threshing Machine King refers to Jerome Increase Case. Pa tells the story that Mr. Case first came to Rochester, Wisconsin, because he felt that it was the middle of the bread basket of America. However, when he asked the village fathers for access to the power provided by the local dam, he was denied. The next day, he moved his operation to Racine. His name was legend in our county since the day he burned one of his machines to the ground! Pa said that Mr. Pynaker in the western part of the county couldn't get his Case threshing machine to work. Mr. Case came out, and he couldn't get it to work either. He burned the wooden machine to the ground and gave the man a new machine! The name Case has been golden ever since.

Let's get back to the cooperation necessary to operate a threshing machine. A group of ten to twelve farmers would get together and share one threshing machine and steam engine. In our case, Emil Wilkes owns the machines and the rest of the farmers pay him for the use of the machine. In Yorkville, getting the farmers together was rather easy since almost all of us share a common origin; our ancestors all originated from Cornwall. Pa told me that Cornwall is a county in England, and the people there are known for their mining abilities and for plundering goods off ships that wash up on their rocky shore. In fact, he said that most people think that Wisconsin is the Badger State because of the badgers that were abundant when the white man first arrived. Not true! Wisconsin is called the Badger State because these Cornish miners looked like a bunch of badgers as they crawled in and out of their lead mines in southwestern Wisconsin.

Let me tell you why it takes so many people to operate these machines. First, a binder is used to cut the grain and tie it into small bundles. Then, about ten of these are grouped together in the field in what is called a shock. After a couple of days to dry, the bundles are loaded onto a wagon. Now we are ready for the threshing machine. The machine usually arrives the day before the threshing is to begin. It is a slow process because the steam engine only goes two miles per hour. The steam engine is connected to the threshing machine by means of a belt about six inches wide and fifty feet long. My brother Walt says that when the machine is running, the belt moves at twenty-eight feet per second. (Walt thinks of himself as a mathematician.) The operator of the steam engine, usually the owner, arrives about 5:00 a.m. to get a fire going in the steam engine and to build up the needed steam pressure. Then, the bundles are fed into the threshing machine by two men alternating putting the bundles into the thresher. One man keeps an eye on the threshing machine and directs the straw into a nearby pile. Several men bag the grain into special Bemis bags and carry these bags to the granary. Bemis bags are made of material similar to canvas and have the company name, as well as the farmer's name, stenciled on them. Everybody used them because the company guaranteed them for life. Often, another group of men would shovel the grain into the proper place in the granary. Plus, more men are busy feeding wood into the steam engine and bringing water to be converted into steam.

The women folk are needed too. Ma and my sister, Mame, have to fix a great dinner for all the workers. This is important for several reasons. One is the bragging rights of being the best cook in Yorkville. Second, if word gets around that the food isn't good, farmers don't want to come and help, and if they do come, they are in a big hurry to move on to the next farm where the food is better.

On the positive side, harvest time is one of the few times when farmers get to talk to their neighbors who often live miles away. So despite the hard work, harvest time is something that farmers and their families usually look forward to.

But even at the best of times, harvesting is nail-biting time. Will the weather be right? Will the machines work properly? Will everybody come and help as they are supposed to? Will the meal be ready on time? Okay, you get the idea. Earlier, I said this year was rough; let me tell you how rough.

Farmers always argue about who gets their crops harvested first. So lately we've been going in alphabetical order one year and reverse alphabetical order the next. This year, we followed reverse alphabetical order. Some of the farmers in our group were Skewes, Vivian, Shepherd, Moyle, Foxwell, Wilkes, Whitley, and a few others I cannot remember. So in reverse alphabetical order this year, we were close to last. This means our crop was getting overly ripe, and the chance of a storm ruining our crop grew larger every day. Pa was getting plenty nervous. Before we could thresh our oats, we needed to help the farmer just before us, the Moyles, and get our oats cut with the binder. Here's how it went.

"Pa, I'm sixteen. It's about time you let me cut the oats," I stated firmly.

Pa replied, "You're too young, plus the field is right by the road, so if you screw up, everybody in Yorkville will be laughing at me."

Pa was referring to the fact that if you weren't careful cutting the grain, you could leave some grain standing or plug the binder up and leave a whole lot standing. Farmers are very proud of how their fields look in comparison to their neighbors'.

Brother Ben piped up, "Pa, let him do it, you know you need my help over at the Moyles'."

Walt added, "Pa, I agree with Ben, you need our help."

I didn't know it then, but Ben and Walt had an ulterior motive. It seemed a rumor had gotten around that the widow Benson, who lived next door to the Moyles', did her farm chores in the nude. I know this sounds unbelievable, but you may also know that young men are foolish in this regard. Both of my brothers wanted to be there, just in case the rumor turned out to be true.

Pa finally agreed, and I was beyond excited to show Pa and the family that I could do a man's job. So the next morning, I was up at dawn. Luckily, there was no morning dew because, if there had been, the bundles would have gotten moldy. I did my chores as quickly as I could, and then I carefully hooked our workhorses, George and Abraham, up to the binder and headed for the field. I had one great fear, the knotter. The knotter was the gizmo that tied the bundles with twine, and no one I knew really understood how it works. I was told it was invented in Wisconsin by a Mr. Appleby, but Pa simply called it a cantankerous invention of the devil. He called it that because it often stopped tying with no apparent reason. I opened the wooden gate to the field and very carefully cut the field of oats. Several times the binder plugged up, but I quickly stopped and unplugged the binder. I know it sounds like bragging, but I did a great job and the knotter worked beautifully. I spent the next five hours putting the bundles into shocks, and those shocks were perfect, if I say so myself. I walked back to the barn, saddled my horse, Toby, and rode over to the Moyles'.

As I arrived at the Moyles', it was about quarter to five. Ben and Walt were feeding the bundles into the thresher. Being late in the day, the bundles were getting a little damp, and the threshing machine was struggling to handle them. I don't know if it was because Ben and Walt were tired or if it was because they were looking over at the widow Benson. Either way, they screwed up, and instead of alternating feeding the bundles, they threw in both bundles at the same time. There was a tremendous bang, and the belt jumped off the pulley, knocking Mr. Moyle to the ground with blood streaming from his forehead. Everyone ran to his side, and Pa took his shirt off and tried to stop the bleeding. Eventually Mr. Moyle came to and the bleeding slowed.

Pa said quietly, "Are you okay, Bob?"

Bob stammered, "I, I, I think so."

Pa turned to Ben and Walt. "What the hell did you do?"

Ben answered, "I'm sorry, Pa. I guess we got out of sync and fed two bundles at once."

Pa snapped, "Apologize to this man!"

Shortly after Ben and Walt apologized, and it seemed like Mr. Moyle was going to be okay, we all rode our horses home. As we approached home, I couldn't wait for Pa to see the great job I had done with the oats. As we got closer, I heard Pa yell, "Damn you, Tom, you didn't shut the gate!" Sure enough, the cows were in the oats field, eating the oats and knocking the shocks to kingdom come. I had never felt so small as my pride in a job well done evaporated. Pa had one more thing to say, "Tom, you'll pay for this!"

I spent the remaining daylight getting the cows out of the field, shutting the gate, and trying, as best as I could, to get the shocks back to some sort of normalcy. The next day, Pa, Walt, and Ben helped finish threshing Mr. Moyle's oats. Nobody was talking to me, and I spent more time straightening the shocks.

The following day, Friday, the steam engine and thresher were due at our place. Sure enough, about two, we saw the steam engine puffing along at two miles per hour, pulling the threshing machine. As it was

JAMES R. VYVYAN SR.

approaching, we were loading the bundles onto a wagon pulled by George and Abraham. Saturday was to be the day of our threshing.

Sure enough, Emil Wilkes arrived early Saturday morning and fed some oak logs into the steam engine and began to build up steam. Ma and Mame were so busy, we had to fend for ourselves for breakfast. Mame was frying chickens in lard. Ma was making apple pies. Together they were making potato salad. The scent was delicious! About ten o'clock, the rest of the crew started to trickle in, and Emil Wilkes started up the threshing machine. Everything went smoothly. Even Mr. Moyle showed up and seemed to be doing a little work, but he had a big bandage around his head, half hidden by his hat. Everybody said that Ma and Mame had the best meal of the whole season, and I overheard the following:

"How many acres of oats did you have?" asked Mr. Wilkes.

"Oh, about six, I guess."

"Six acres, huh?" replied Mr. Wilkes, and you could tell he was thinking. "You know, I think you had the best yield of anyone this year!"

I could tell Pa was astounded as he said sheepishly, "Really?"

Later that night, Pa came into my bedroom. "Tom, are you awake?"

"Yes, Pa."

"You screwed up with that gate, but we're just going to forget the whole thing."

As he left, I thought he could have told me about the big yield or at least about the good job I had done cutting the oats. Oh well, life goes on, and praise is in short supply.

CHAPTER THREE

County Fair

THE RACINE COUNTY Fair has been a popular event for generations. Its location has been in flux. It's been located at Highway 45 and Highway A in Yorkville, Burlington, Taylor Avenue in Racine, and Highway 11 in Union Grove. The location doesn't really matter; it is one of the few times when we get to meet people and have some real fun. Let me tell you about this year's fair.

It started in June, when a sign was posted at McQuarry's General Store. The sign read as follows:

Racine County Fair

August 3

10:00 AM	Opening Ceremony
11:00 AM	Apple Pie Judging
1:00 PM	Sulky Race
2:00 PM	Pulling Contest
3:00 PM	Farmer's Plug Race
4:00 PM	Game Time
	Greased Pig Contest
	Greased Pole Contest
	Cow Chip Toss
5:00 PM	Closing Ceremony

Brother Ben saw the sign first and brought the news to the rest of the family. My sister, Mame, promptly challenged Ma to the apple pie contest. The sulky race held little interest for our family. There are a couple of reasons for this. First, let me explain a sulky race.

A sulky is a small, light two-wheeled vehicle pulled by a single horse. There are two kinds of sulky races: trotter and pacer. I can never remember the difference, but Ben tells me a trotter moves his or her right front leg and right rear leg together. A pacer moves their right front and left rear leg in unison.

So why aren't we interested in the sulky race? Two reasons: First, the horse can't be just any horse. It's practically a must that the horse only be used for trotting or pacing. Few farmers can afford to have a horse that is used only a couple of days a year. Second, a while back, Jerome Increase Case had a horse called Jay Eye See. This horse wasn't only a good trotter; he held the world's record at two minutes and ten seconds for the mile. How could any local farmer beat a world champion? Mr. Case continues to have world-quality trotters and pacers, so the sulky race isn't really a race at all. It should be called Mr. Case Wins.

Next up is the pulling contest. This event could be called Mr. Whitley Wins. Mr. Whitley has a team of horses that he refers to as Hercules and Samson. These horses must weigh close to a ton each, and frankly, nobody else has a chance. Therefore, there are usually only one or two entries beyond Mr. Whitley, and those are farmers who have never heard about Mr. Whitley and his horses.

Now here comes the exciting event, the farmers' plug race. This race was created to counteract the way Mr. Case dominates the sulky race. The farmers' plug race is exactly what it says. The only people allowed to enter are those who make a living by farming. Mr. Case and the other townsfolk aren't allowed to enter. I know I've told you before that I fancied that my horse, Toby, was the fastest horse in Yorkville. However, this is the *county* fair; there would be horses from far and wide. I wasn't sure how Toby would fare, but I was excited.

The fair finishes with games. I definitely wasn't interested in the cow chip toss. I'm not squeamish, but throwing cow poop doesn't really excite me. I have mixed feelings about the greased pig and greased pole contest. We'll see.

So we had two months to think and dream about the possibilities at the fair. I tried to exercise Toby as much as possible. Plus, you may remember last year's fair where Linda said "Hello" to me and all I could say was "Ah . . . ah . . . ah, I gotta go." If I get the opportunity this year, I am going to do better. I have even planned what I will say if I get the chance.

Fair Day

I jumped out of bed at the crack of dawn, and the day seemed to be starting out bright and sunny. I got my chores done at breakneck speed, had a little breakfast, and saddled Toby. I thought I'd stop at McQuarry's store and get some of my favorite Wrigley's chewing gum. I figured I could probably get it at the fair, but it would certainly be more expensive. As I stepped in the store, I recognized Mr. Whitley. "Hi, Mr. Whitley, I'll bet you're going to win the pulling contest."

"I don't think so, Tom. Hercules has foundered. I was feeding Hercules and Samson extra grain to build them up for the pulling contest, and I guess I overdid it. Hercules can barely walk, and my boys are applying a mud poultice right about now."

"You mean your team won't be at the pulling contest?"

"I'm afraid not, Tom."

As I left the store, I got to thinking. I was familiar with a horse foundering; it happened to one of our horses. It is usually caused by overeating rich feed. I can understand Mr. Whitley trying to build up his horses, but he really didn't need to; when healthy, his horses were unbeatable. As I understand it, the rich food causes a swelling and pain in the hoof of the horse. The standard treatment is a combination of mud poultices, having the horse stand in mud, and encouraging the horse to spend time lying down. The condition takes a long time to heal, and sometimes the horse has to be destroyed.

Wait just a minute! I might be the only one who knew Samson and Hercules wouldn't be competing in the pulling contest; therefore, any good team had a chance. I immediately turned around and headed back to the farm. I explained the situation to Pa, harnessed George and Abraham, and headed to the fair with Toby tied behind.

By the time I reached the fair, the sulky race was already in progress. It was hard to tell who was in the lead. I asked one of the spectators, and he said that Case's horse had just lapped the field. Just like I thought, the race could be called Mr. Case Wins.

Next was the pulling contest. Let me explain how this works: Picture a flat wooden object four feet wide and twelve feet long made out of heavy planks. This is referred to as a stoneboat. It is called a stoneboat because farmers use it to move large stones out of their fields. On the stoneboat, bags of sand are added to make it heavy and hard to pull. Men are lined up and spaced ten feet apart. As the horses pull the stoneboat, every ten feet a man steps on making it harder and harder to pull. Eventually the horses can no longer pull the stoneboat, and the distance that they have pulled is measured. Whichever team pulls it the farthest wins.

My guess was correct, and there were only two other teams entered in the pulling contest. I was first and carefully hooked George and Abraham to the stoneboat. There must have been two hundred people cheering and yelling. I clicked my tongue and shouted "Go!" George and Abraham pulled just like I knew they would, and they pulled for a total of 136 feet. Next up was Joe Symoens. Joe's team was smaller than George and Abraham's, so I felt pretty confident. They only pulled eighty-seven feet. One more to go. This team was huge, almost as big as Mr. Whitley's team. They were owned and driven by Mr. Garbe. Mr. Garbe clicked his tongue, and his team moved their feet a little but didn't pull at all. Mr. Garbe tried again—nothing. It seemed like the horses were frightened by all the cheering spectators. He tried one more time—nothing. I won! I won! I can't believe I won!

People I didn't even know were patting me on the back and pumping my hand. Wow! Just then Linda appeared out of nowhere with a big smile and yelled, "Congratulations, Tom!"

I replied, "It's so good to see you. I really had a good time at your party, and I've put a frame on the picture you gave me." (This was my response I had rehearsed.) With that, Linda smiled and disappeared again into the crowd.

So far so good, but now it's time for the farmers' plug race. I mounted Toby and headed for the starting line. The race was five times around the track. There were eleven young men entered, and it looked as though they ranged in age from twelve to midtwenties. I knew three of them: my friend Joe Maranger, who was riding his horse Dobbin; neighbor Dave Nafziger; and a guy I knew from church, Matthew. (I can't remember his last name.)

The gun went off, and Toby and I jumped into the lead. As we finished the first lap, I was first, followed by someone I didn't know, and then by Joe Maranger. Then something happened that I didn't expect. Toby started to slow down, and his breathing seemed labored. Then it dawned on me. I was so busy with the pulling contest, I had left Toby in the hot sun with no water for the last two hours! Shit! I'm losing, and it's my fault! I don't mind losing so much, but the fact that it's my fault really bugs me. The race ended, and I was dead last. I was happy to congratulate the winner, my friend Joe.

I watered Toby and walked him around to cool him off. Meanwhile, I was keeping an eye on the greased pole contest. Contestant after contestant tried to climb the twelve-foot greased pole to get the ten-dollar bill at the top. I tied Toby under a big oak and noticed that the climbers were getting a little higher. I guess some of the grease was wearing off. After thirty minutes, still no one had gotten to the top. Judging the contest was Mr. Huck. I said, "Mr. Huck, what are the rules of this contest?"

"Well, I don't believe anyone has bothered to write down any rules, young man. The first person to the top gets the money."

I'm an honest young man, but I had an idea. I called for my friend Joe, and I climbed on his shoulders, and within seconds, I had the ten dollars! Mr. Huck smiled and said, "Well, I'll be goldarned, I never did see such a thing." I split the ten dollars with Joe and the fair was over.

So that's the Racine County Fair. I have bragging rights for having the best team of horses in the county! I screwed up with Toby, and my response to Linda was lame but better than last year. I'm five dollars richer, and by the way, Mame got first place for her apple pie. Mame can do anything.

CHAPTER FOUR

Winter

WINTER ON THE farm is a time to do the chores, fix the machines, and milk the cows. In short, winter on the farm is boring. This winter has been an exception.

One morning, shortly after Christmas, Pa told my brothers, Ben and Walt, to meet him in the dining room. Pa told me to get there too! We knew something big was up. Pa started in, "Boys, I've been giving a lot of thought to the future. I'm in my fifties, and I won't be around forever. Do you boys want to spend your life farming?"

In turn, we all responded, "Yes, Pa."

"Then we've got a problem. This farm isn't big enough for all of us. Walt and Ben, you've been asking for more money for the work you do around here. You're both in your twenties. It's time for a change. Here's what I'm thinking, I'll put a mortgage of $4,000 on the home farm and put a $2,000 down payment on the Ferber farm for Walt and a $2,000 down payment on the Jensen farm for Ben."

I jumped in with, "What about me, Pa?"

"When I die, the home farm will be yours, probably with a sizeable mortgage. I want you all to think about this, and we'll meet again tomorrow morning."

We were all pretty much speechless. Each of us would have our own farm. Each of us would have a mortgage. Then it dawned on me, what about our sister, Mame? My brothers and I talked, and we all felt it was pretty fair to each of us. One of our questions was—what would Walt and Ben do for equipment? Another question was—how soon will this happen?

The next morning, we gathered again in the dining room. This time, Ma and Mame joined us. Pa began, "Let's talk this through. I think we all know the basic plan. Walt will have the Ferber farm, Ben the Jensen farm, and upon my death, Tom will have the home farm. I might add, each of you will have a sizeable mortgage."

I piped up, "What about Mame?"

Ma answered, "Mame will get $250 when Pa and I die. That is a lot of money. Plus, Mame will eventually be getting married, and she'll have a husband to take care of her."

Mame is usually very quiet and meek, so I was surprised when she angrily responded, "I'm as much a part of this family as the boys! They get $2,000, and I get $250, that's just not fair!"

Pa said firmly, "Now you know as well as I that farms are always passed down from man to man. You mind your place!"

I wanted to jump in and defend Mame's position, but something held me back.

Ben didn't seem to care and wondered, "What will Walt and I do for equipment? We each have a little money but not nearly enough to buy all the equipment we'll need."

Pa replied, "We can share equipment for the first couple years. All the farms are within a mile of one another, so sharing equipment seems workable."

Walt asked, "When will this happen?"

"I've talked to Mr. Ferber, Mr. Jensen, and the bank. I believe we can have everything set before spring planting."

So it was settled. Everyone in the family started thinking about how things were going to change. My first thought was, if Walt and Ben have their own farms, far more work is going to fall on my shoulders. I'll have to talk to Pa about an increase in wages.

You could tell that a major shift had taken place in the family. Walt and Ben spent a lot of time planning how they were going to run their farms. I also noticed they spent a lot of Saturday nights with the young people's group at church. It didn't seem like they were planning to live alone on their new farms. The biggest change was in Mame. She was no longer so meek and subservient to Ma and Pa. She told me that it was clear she couldn't depend on Ma and Pa, and she was set on making a life for herself.

While this was happening, all the regular chores still had to be done. One of the most interesting jobs was ice harvesting. The only way we kept our food cold was the kitchen icebox. Twice a week, the icebox was fueled with a chunk of ice weighing about eighty pounds. This meant that spring, summer, winter, and fall we had to have a supply of these eighty-pound chunks of ice.

Let me explain how this works. First, an icehouse is needed to store the ice until needed. We didn't have such a thing, but luckily, just up the street, Walter Vivian had a big one. An icehouse is a building that is double-walled with the space between the walls filled with sawdust. This serves as insulation to keep the ice from melting during the spring and summer.

Second, you needed a source of ice. My brother Walt says you can harvest one thousand tons of ice from one acre of a lake or pond. You may remember, Walt fancies himself a mathematician. So really, it doesn't take a very large body of water to provide the ice.

Third, you needed a large group of workers because a lot of labor is needed to get the ice from the pond to the icehouse. These workers wait until the ice is at least ten inches thick; otherwise, the teams of horses might fall through the ice. Then, one worker hooks a scraper behind his team and scrapes the snow off the ice. Another worker hooks his team to the ice plow. The ice plow scores the ice. This means that it makes one-inch-deep grooves every twenty-two inches both north and south and east and west. The result is a pond that looks like a checker board. Then workers saw the ice along the grooves, separating the ice into blocks. The blocks are pushed and pulled up a wooden ramp onto a wagon. The wagon is used to haul the blocks of ice to the icehouse where the ice is unloaded and packed with sawdust.

Ice harvesting is one of a few social occasions, kind of like threshing time. Gathering in early February were the Foxwells, Skewes, Moyles, Whitleys, Wilkes, Nafzigers, Vivians, Marangers, and the Hucks. Plus, there was a newcomer, Allen Gorzky and his son Edwin.

The boss of this operation was Mr. Moyle because the pond was on his property. I've been hesitant to tell you about the worst job in harvesting ice. This job is called the shine boy, and up until two years ago, it was my job. You may remember the ice chunks are put in the icebox to keep our food cool. The horses that work on the ice aren't particularly sanitary. In fact they poop and piss whenever the spirit moves them. It is the job of the shine boy to clean up the poop and the piss and treat that area of the ice with formaldehyde. I think you can see why it is considered the worst and lowest job.

As we gathered early on Thursday morning, Mr. Moyle assigned the jobs. Pa was assigned the job of pulling the ice plow. Walt, Ben, and I were assigned the job of sawing the ice. Edwin Gorzky was assigned the job of shine boy.

Edwin was twelve years old, but he was as tall as I was. He was a handsome boy, but his smile was kinda crooked, and it gave me the willies. As soon as we started to work, he came up to me and said, "I guess you won't be pasturing your heifers on the Vanswol farm!" I knew something about this. We had pastured our young heifers on the Vanswol farm for as long as I could remember. Every spring, we would drive our heifers over to the Vanswol woods, where they would spend the summer eating the grass among the oak trees. The Gorzkys had offered to double the rent we had been paying. This is considered "not neighborly" and is usually not done. I simply responded to Edwin by saying, "I guess you're right."

We all started to do our jobs. I enjoyed sawing the ice. It was hard work and similar to sawing wood, but each stroke of the saw cut a good inch of ice. I could easily see my progress which felt good. As I was sawing, occasionally a snowball would come my way. It usually missed, but Pa had taught me that work time was not a time for Tom Foolery, so I didn't respond. All of a sudden, I felt a hand pushing snow down the back of my neck. Out of instinct, I pulled at the perpetrator, and before I knew it, Edwin was in the water.

Did I tell you that it was near zero today? Edwin started yelling, "You pushed me in! You pushed me in! Damn you!" There was no danger of Edwin drowning since the pond wasn't more than four feet deep.

Edwin's pa was now yelling at my pa, "What the hell has your son done?"

Pa didn't take the bait and simply said, "We've got to get him warm and dry."

Pa and Edwin's pa pulled him out of the water, and his pa took him home before he froze.

We kept on working, but I could tell there were eyes on me. When we got home, Pa wanted to know what had really happened. I told him about the snowballs and the snow down my neck. He didn't hesitate, "I knew it wasn't your fault, Tom, but it would be best if you kept your distance from Edwin Gorzky."

JAMES R. VYVYAN SR.

CHAPTER FIVE

Spring

I'M NO LONGER shy, and I find it easy to talk to girls. Oh, did I tell you it's April Fool's Day?

Seriously, a lot has happened in the last few months. My brothers, Walt and Ben, are getting married! It seems that young, handsome men who own a farm are quite a catch. Also, Walt and Ben surely didn't want to live alone on their new farms. Walt is engaged to Elizabeth Brown from the Town of Raymond, and Ben is engaged to Florence Showalter from Union Grove. We've all known both girls for many years since they belong to our church.

The weddings present a minor problem—what to do for presents? Mame and I have been talking this over. Neither Walt nor Ben has a buggy or carriage; if they travel, they ride their horses. Neither Walt nor Ben is able to afford such since they have so many things to buy to furnish their new homes and equip their farms. I noticed that Mr. Jensen was having an auction, and he had two broken down buggies to sell. On auction day, Mame and I went to the sale. We got the first one for $10.50 and the second for $7.25.

These buggies sure needed work. On the first one, I replaced an axle and fashioned a new single tree. (A single tree is where the harness is attached to the buggy.) On the second buggy, the floor was rotten, so I replaced the floor with some sturdy oak boards we had on hand. Meantime, Mame reupholstered both seats. I told you, Mame can do anything. Finally, working together, we painted them both with a nice black paint. When we were done, they looked like new! We couldn't wait for the wedding, so when the couples came to our farm for the engagement dinner, we presented them with the buggies. They were all mighty surprised and pleased. Ben's fiancée said, "You couldn't have gotten us a more perfect gift. I was afraid I'd have to ride a horse to church." Walt's fiancée, Liz, gave us both big smiles and hugs.

The weddings went off as planned. They were small affairs and not much fun for a sixteen-year-old boy. Pa and Ma gave each couple six bred heifers for a wedding present so that they would have some regular income from the milk. Plus, since they were bred heifers, they would soon have a herd of twelve Holsteins.

But now the house seems really empty. It is just the four of us: Ma, Pa, Mame, and me. Plus, now I'm called for milking twice a day, seven days a week. One thing has us all a little worried. Last year, we had one farm with 150 acres and four men to work the farm. Now we have three hundred acres and three farms! How are we going to manage? Ben and Walt had the good sense to each buy a team of horses. There was no way our team, George and Abraham, could handle all three farms.

As planting season approaches, I've been thinking about the tremendous competition that exists between farmers. Who has the best looking and best producing cows? Who has the best field of corn, wheat, or hay? In the past, it was common for Ma, Pa, and me to go for a Sunday ride just to look at the competition. And if it looked like our crops were the best, we'd be busting our britches with pride. It dawned on me that now that competition would include Ben and Walt.

In talking with Pa, it seems that he too is worried about how the two of us will handle all the work that four of us handled last year. Just as it was time to start the spring plowing, a minor disaster struck. Pa got the gout. His left big toe was red and swollen. Pa said it felt like there was a fire burning in that big toe. He could barely walk. He was able to sit on a milk stool and milk the cows, but he wasn't good for much else. Oh boy, now what are we going to do?

Here I am, sixteen, and I have nearly full responsibility for a 150-acre farm. I'm feeling the pressure, but I am bound and determined to make the farm hum. The first job is to plow the fields with George and Abraham. This is tough work. I walk behind the one bottom plow, with the reins over my shoulders and my hands on the handles of the plow. George and Abraham are well-trained, and once started, they don't need much direction. However, if the plow hits a rock, the plow will twist violently, and it feels like my arms are about to break.

I don't want to give you the idea that plowing is all bad. Horses can't plow continually; every few rounds, they need a rest. When they rest, I rest. I might just lie in the lush grass and dream about Linda and what I'd say to her, or do with her, if I wasn't so shy. Or I might chase a rabbit, or I might take a little snooze, or I might just gaze at the blue sky overhead. Like I said, plowing is not all bad. Still, after a long day walking behind the plow, I'm dead tired and my arms ache.

The next step is to work the field with a disk or a spring tooth. This is my first real problem. There is tremendous pressure to get the work done since I'm the only one working. However, if you work our clay ground too wet, it will bake like a stone and nothing will grow. So I pick up a handful and take it back to show Pa. Course, even this is a problem because I could pick a handful from a dry spot or a wet spot. I imagine how I'll feel if I do this wrong and we don't have a crop this fall. Somehow I get the fields worked.

Now it's time for planting. First, I plant the oats because a frost won't hurt the oats. In fact, the earlier the oats are planted, the better. Second, I plant the corn. This is my next problem. Generally, the earlier you plant the corn the better, but if you plant it too early and it freezes, you could lose the whole crop. What to do? What to do? So I talk with Pa, and he tells me to take a ride and see what the neighbors are doing. I first ride to Ben's place, and then Walt's place, and three of us take a ride through the country. We find the Skewes are planting corn and so are the Vivians. However, the Moyles say it is way too early. We go back and report our findings to Pa. Pa suggests we get everything ready and start tomorrow. So as I begin to plant the corn, my next problem presents itself. How deep should I plant the corn? If I plant it too shallow, the seed won't germinate and just lie there. If I plant it too deep, there won't be enough oomph in the seed to push the corn plant all the way to the surface. Complicating matters for me is that in some places, the ground is hard and that affects the depth too. Decisions! Decisions!

As I'm finishing this chapter, it is July 4. I walk through the cornfields and nearly all the corn is knee-high—knee-high by the fourth of July. I put Toby on the buggy and take Pa for a ride to see our corn and the neighbors' corn. We come home with huge smiles on our faces. Walt's and Ben's fields are good too.

Is this the end? No, but perhaps it is the end of the beginning. We still have to worry about too much or too little rain. We still have to worry about hail and insects and an early fall frost. Although I'm aware of all these possibilities, for the moment, I'm as happy as a pup with two tails.

CHAPTER SIX

Linda

SIX YEARS HAVE passed since Linda and I shared our sixteenth birthday. You may remember she gave me a hand-drawn picture of me and my horse, Toby. I need to bring you up to date on Linda. I'll go back to a time shortly after our birthdays.

After our sixteenth birthdays, I tried to think of some way to have further contact with Linda. She was going to Union Grove High School, and I was working on the farm. I finally had a plan. If I made a frame for the picture she gave me, certainly it wouldn't be too unusual to show it to her. So I did. I made what I thought was a beautiful wooden frame for the picture and saddled up and headed for Linda's house. I was really shy about this, so I rode by her house hoping to see her outside. Nothing. I rode by again with the same result. I turned around and rode by her house a third time, but this time, I stopped and went to the door. I gently knocked, and her father came to the door. "Is Linda home?"

"No, she and her mother are at church."

There was something in the way that he said those words, something cold. I'm not used to that, virtually everybody likes me. I'm polite, honest, and fairly well dressed. It was a puzzle, but I replied, "Thank you, sir."

As I rode home, I thought to myself, I'm not going to try that again. So my next plan was to time my trips to Union Grove with the bell ending the school day. Pa thought I was making my usual trip to get some lime for the barn. I was slowly passing by school just as the bell rang, and I tried to look for Linda without looking like I was looking for Linda. There she was, walking with a girl I didn't know, so I just waved and yelled "Hi." She waved back. A few weeks later, I found another excuse to go to Union Grove, but this time I actually stopped, tied up the horses, and waited for Linda to get out of school. This was a really big step for me. Would she be glad to see me? Would she ignore me and walk past? Finally, the bell rang, and she walked out alone. "Hi, Linda!"

"Hi yourself, Tom."

"I just wanted to show you the frame I made for the picture you gave me."

And so it went each time I went to Union Grove, we talked a little longer, and each time my confidence in me and in Linda grew.

I never did tell Linda about the time I talked to her father. If she knew about it, she never mentioned it. Eventually, graduation time arrived. Linda was graduating from high school. This was a big event; no one in our family had ever gone to high school—much less graduated. Again, I thought and thought about what kind of present to get her. I ended up buying a small jewelry box and had Mame use her calligraphy skills to put a big *L* on the lid.

There were seven graduates, and Linda was the valedictorian. She gave a wonderful speech about how we can make the future a better place. I met her as she was returning her robe to the principal. "I have something for you, Linda."

"That's so sweet, Tom." She slowly unwrapped the jewelry box, and for the first time, she gave me a hug. I thought my heart was going to burst.

"What are you going to do now, Linda?"

"My math teacher has encouraged me to enroll in Miss Brown's Business College in Milwaukee."

My mind instantly began to wonder how, or when, I would see her if she enrolled. It would take about four hours to get to Milwaukee on horseback and four hours back. I was able to get out, "That sounds great."

Off she went to Milwaukee. We communicated by letters at least once a week. Our letters slowly grew in warmth, and by spring, she signed one of her letters, "Love, Linda." I read that letter over a hundred times and each time enjoyed it as much as the first. I asked Pa if I could borrow the buggy for a day. The answer was "If you got your work done, and any day but Sunday." Sunday, of course, was when the family used it to go to church. I planned a trip to visit Milwaukee and hoped for a beautiful day. Finally, the day arrived, and it was a warm and sunny day. I hurried through my chores, harnessed Toby to the buggy, and off I went.

Linda lived in an apartment reserved for young women. It was on Wisconsin Avenue not far from the grand house of Frederick Pabst. I knocked on the door, and it was answered by an older woman. "Is Linda Shunk available?"

"I'll let her know she has a visitor."

Just then, Linda came down the stairs with the biggest smile I've ever seen. If anything, she was more beautiful than ever. She wore a white blouse with a blue checked skirt.

"What shall we do?"

"Let's go to the lakefront, Tom."

Linda had packed a lunch and off we went. We took off our shoes and strolled along the beach. The water was as blue as blue can be with a number of three-masted schooners with billowing white sails. Linda surprised me when she turned to me, looked me in the eyes, and said, "I love you, Tom." She further surprised me when she kissed me on the lips in a soft and tender way that I had only dreamed of. It was my first kiss.

Her lunch was delicious, but before I knew it, I found myself saying, "I've gotta go home and do chores." I could have stayed longer, but I was afraid I would say or do something that would ruin this perfect day. We had a few similar days in the three years she was at Miss Brown's College; they were all good, but none as good as that first one.

Now, as graduation was approaching, I wanted to take the lead. So far, Linda was the first at everything. The first to give a personal gift— the drawing, the first to say I love you, the first to initiate a hug, and the first to give a kiss. I'm twenty-two years old. I'm a man. It's time. I talked to Mame, and together we picked out an engagement ring. The Saturday before graduation, I arranged to pick Linda up in Milwaukee. I took her to what I had heard was the best restaurant in town, the Pfister. We had a wonderful meal and delightful conversation, and at the end, I swallowed hard and simply said, "Will you marry me?" To which she replied, "Well, of course, silly, I thought you would never ask!"

We planned to tell her parents the following Sunday. As the day approached, my anxiety continued to rise. Of course, I'd seen her pa a few times over the years, but I never felt any warmth from the man. Sunday eventually arrived, and I sat down with the Shunks for dinner. As we finished dinner, according to plan, Linda and I rose holding hands. "Mr. and Mrs. Shunk, I have asked and Linda has accepted my proposal of marriage, and we seek your blessing."

JAMES R. VYVYAN SR.

There was a long pause. Finally, Mr. Shunk spoke, "I respect you, Tom. I know you are a hardworking, honest, and decent man. However, we cannot give you our blessing, for you are not Catholic. The Bible states that a couple should be equally yoked."

I had thought about this and had always said to myself, "I'll convert." So I said, "Mr. Shunk, I love Linda, and I will convert for her."

"Do you know what you are saying? Are you willing to accept the pope as God on earth? Are you willing to accept the wine and bread of communion as the actual body of Christ?"

"I, ah . . . ah . . ."

He continued, "Why don't you go home and think this through."

With that, Linda and I walked outside, and I left with Linda saying, "We'll find a way."

I sat down with Ma, Pa, and Mame and explained the situation. Pa is the only one that spoke. "Tom, you know that we are Protestants and Methodists and have been for generations. Do you know what it means to be Protestant?"

"No, sir."

"The word *Protestant* comes from the word *protesting*, protesting against the Catholic Church. You've mentioned believing that the wine and bread of communion are the actual body of Christ. Isn't that cannibalism? Could you really believe that a man, like you and me, is a god on earth? Have you thought about raising your children in the Catholic Church? They allow drinking, dancing, and gambling. We've always believed those things to be sins. Furthermore, if you continue in this folly, we will not attend the ceremony."

I was devastated; I didn't know what to do. My head was filled with so many thoughts; I thought it would explode. I rode over to Linda's, and we sat under the big oak in her backyard. "My folks say they won't attend our marriage if I convert to Catholicism. What would happen if you converted to Methodist?"

"I spoke to Pa about this, and he said he would disown me."

Tears flowed, and we hugged each other.

A week later, a box arrived containing the engagement ring and a simple note, "Dear Tom, I love you with all my heart, but both of us know that it can never work, Linda."

Six months later, Linda and my friend Joe Maranger were married in the Catholic Church.

CHAPTER SEVEN

The Black Dog

I 'M NOT SURE I can explain how I feel. It's beyond sadness. I hear and see my surroundings, but it's like I'm not part of it. I feel like an observer rather than a participant of life. I don't go anywhere except to church on Sunday. I have no interest in seeing another woman. In fact, I don't have any interest in women at all. The best times, if you can call them that, is when I'm really working hard. When the sweat is rolling down my arms and cascading off my forehead, I almost feel a part of the world. I'm not sure someone who has not experienced it can comprehend what I'm feeling.

The worst times are at night when the work is done. In the past, I would use these times to read or work on fun projects. I have no interest in either. When I climb into bed, I lie there, and sleep refuses to come. The lack of sleep contributes to my condition. The rest of the family tried really hard for a while to bring me out of this. Now I think they feel as if they have done all they can. I get the impression they are trying to avoid me.

Now a new problem, Ma has obviously been losing weight. At first I thought she was feeling my pain, but now I can see it is much, much more. Doc Moyle has been called, but nobody tells me anything. I think I heard the word *cancer* whispered between Pa and Doc.

On a positive note, our crops are among the best, if not the best, in Yorkville. The four of us took a ride through the countryside today, and it was confirmed. We came home with smiles, Ma included.

Speaking of Ma, she has more and more taken to her bed. Mame has taken over most of her jobs. Today, Ma called me into their bedroom. "Tom, I've got to talk with you. I know just telling you to snap out of it is not enough. My pa had something similar, he called it the Black Dog, and he fought it through a good part of his life. You had a terrible thing happen to you, but you need to know that our family has a tendency for the Black Dog. You've got to fight it. You've got to get out and make a life for yourself. It may seem impossible. Maybe for the time being, if you just act like you enjoy life, someday you actually will."

The next morning, she was gone, and it was just the three of us. They say bad things happen in threes. I sure hope that's not true; I can't take a third.

CHAPTER EIGHT

The Canal

A SIZEABLE CHUNK of our farm has always been too wet to produce any crops. The same is true of Walt's and Ben's farms. In fact, darn near every farm in Yorkville had a sizeable piece of ground that is too wet to work. I've been trying to act like my old self, and I have been reading the *Farm Journal*. There was a big article about digging canals. The idea is to use a huge steam shovel to dig a canal (artificial river) to drain the wet acres. Thinking this through and looking at a map of Yorkville, I could envision a canal starting in the northwest part of Yorkville and running diagonally to the southeast part of Yorkville and emptying into the Root River.

The article went on to say that the canal itself was not enough. The canal would certainly help, but without tiles there would still be substantial wetlands. A tile is a tube about one foot long and six inches in diameter made of baked clay. Mr. Nisen, in Union Grove, has begun manufacturing tiles in his huge kiln. The idea is to dig a trench, anywhere from three to five feet deep, starting at the canal and going across the wetland. The tiles are put in the trench end to end. The trench is covered with soil and the water seeps through the ground into the tiles and runs to the canal.

I've been talking about this with neighbors for a year or more, and I've got a few of the younger, more progressive, farmers interested. I even contacted the Wisconsin Secretary of Agriculture. He said that such a project would require the creation of a drainage district. All the farmers whose property would contain part of the canal would have a vote. Majority rules.

The state sent out a team of engineers to draw up a plan for the location and estimated price of the canal. They presented me with the proposed location and a price estimate of $21,000. I almost fell over! Twenty-one thousand dollars is more money than my mind could even comprehend. Walt's farm, Ben's farm, and our farm together weren't worth even close to that number. I talked to Walt about it, and he quickly did some mental arithmetic. "That's a hell of a lot of money, but if you break it down by farm, it would only be about $800 per farm."

I decided I was going to make the canal happen. I began the task of notifying the twenty-six farms that would be involved. I told them there would be a meeting on May 1 at 7:00 p.m. at Yorkville School to vote on a drainage district. I also tried to point out the advantages of the canal. Some people were receptive, some were not. The Gorzkys wouldn't even talk; they just nodded.

I looked forward to the May 1 meeting. Although, personally, I was still struggling, I felt this project might help me get back on track. Finally, the day arrived, and by seven o'clock, the school was full of farmers and some wives. I called the meeting to order and arranged with Matthew Olle to make a motion to approve the creation of the drainage district. I had also arranged for Jon Nafziger to second the motion. Then the discussion began. It basically broke down into the farmers who had only a few acres of wetlands speaking against the project and those with many acres of wetlands being enthusiastic. Finally, the vote came, and Mr. Gorzky asked for a secret ballot. The final tally was thirteen for and ten against with three abstentions. The motion passed! Before the meeting was adjourned I was appointed president; Matt Olle, vice president; and Jon Nafziger, treasurer.

The next week, we put a notice in the Racine paper, asking for bids to dig the drainage canal. We received only two bids, and we interviewed both bidders. The first bidder, Joe Cum, presented himself well enough, but when I asked him how many canals he had dug, the answer was this would be the first. The second bidder, Rocky Chalmers, was a tall well-built ox of a man. I asked him how many canals he had dug. He said three, and his bid was accepted for $20,200.

These were busy times. Not only was I working our farm, but Pa still had trouble with gout and his health was not the best. In addition, I tried to visit the digging as often as I could. It was quite a sight. I had never seen a machine so big and so powerful.

Slowly this machine dug its way across the town, foot by foot, and yard by yard. On a good day, it could dig perhaps one thousand feet of canal. On a bad day, with many stones and a spot where the canal needed to be deeper, it might dig only one hundred feet in a day. At this rate, it would take nearly a year to complete the canal. On July 7, the huge machine came into view from our house. I rode out and asked Rocky to join us for supper. He was only too glad to oblige. He had been living on this machine for four months and cooking his own meals.

That night, Pa, Mame, Rocky, and I sat down to a wonderful meal that Mame had prepared. We had only about three bites when I noticed there was a spark in the air. Something about the way Mame and Rocky looked at each other. After supper, the two of them sat together on the front porch, and I noticed as the days went on that the progress on the canal had slowed considerably. I was pretty sure I knew why. It wasn't long before Mame and Rocky were going to church together each Sunday. I sure understood why Rocky was interested in Mame. Mame is beautiful and can do anything. I'm only surprised that someone hadn't gotten to her sooner. On Sunday, September 17, they announced their engagement. They would be married just before Christmas. I was happy for Mame, but I sure was going to miss her.

CHAPTER NINE

Marriage

MY BEST FRIEND, and sister, is getting married. It is hard to imagine just Pa and me sitting around the table. Hard to imagine what we're going to eat. Hard to imagine not having Mame to talk to.

Last night Rocky joined us for supper. After a great dessert of apple pie and ice cream, Pa had an announcement. "Mame, I know you've never felt it fair that your brothers are getting a farm and you are getting $250. However, part of our thinking was that your mother and I would pay for your wedding. Now that your mother has passed, I still want to pay for your wedding."

Rocky responded, "Mr. Foxwell, that is very kind of you, but I earn good money, and I am more than willing to pay for our wedding."

"Thank you, but I would feel like I'm letting my late wife down if I didn't make good on the agreement we made to each other."

Mame and Rocky in unison said, "Thank you."

It wasn't long after that Mame and Rocky had a plan for the wedding. Mame started, "Pa, our wedding won't be a lavish affair. The wedding will be Saturday, December 17, at 4:00 p.m. at the Yorkville Methodist Church. I'd like the Ladies Society to provide coffee, punch, and cake afterwards. If you could take care of that cost, it would be wonderful. That leaves only one thing. I've always dreamed of being married in a beautiful wedding gown. I mean the kind of dress you can't get at McQuarry's general store or through a catalog. I know this could be considered extravagant, but it's something that would mean the world to me. I've talked to some of my friends, and they have recommended Grace O'Conner to be the seamstress. The way it works is, a month before the wedding, Grace would come and live with us while she works on sewing and fitting the dress. Now, I don't want you to faint, Pa, but she charges $100."

I nearly fell off my chair. One hundred dollars for a dress! Pa's face got red, but he remained calm and simply said, "It would make your mother happy."

Two weeks later, Ms. Grace O'Conner arrived. She was one of the tallest women I've ever met, probably five feet ten inches. Mame was only five feet two or three, and I'm only five feet eight. She had light brown hair, hazel eyes, and a pretty face. I probably shouldn't put this down, but her breasts seemed a wee bit small and she was wearing a blouse that showed just a hint of them.

Meals were more interesting now. Once again, it was four of us at the table. It seems that Grace is Scottish and somehow has a different perspective on life than the Cornish people I'm used to. This makes for interesting conversation. It didn't take long for us to become friends. Her parents are also farmers, and it turns out their farm is totally paid for. I've always heard the Scots have a way with money.

Grace is not afraid of work, and she spends eight to ten hours a day working on the dress. Plus, she finds time to sit on the porch in the evening. I find myself drawn to sit there too.

I haven't thought about a woman in a long time. Grace is now sleeping in the bedroom next to mine, and I have to admit it excites me. I'd forgotten how it feels to be attracted to a woman.

"Grace, I hope that you'll be going to church with the family on Sunday."

"That's mighty nice of you, Tom. You know I come from a Methodist church in Mount Pleasant."

From that first Sunday on, the four of us went to church together, and Grace seemed to prefer sitting next to me.

The thirty days went by quickly. Before I knew it, we were all dressing for the wedding. It's hard for me to describe how Mame looked in her wedding dress. I don't know the words they use in fashion. I only know I've never seen a more beautiful dress in any store, catalog, or magazine. Mame is pretty to begin with, but this dress made her look like a goddess. I could tell Mame was beyond happy. The moment that Rocky saw Mame walking down the aisle was incredible. His face had the look of pure joy.

Of course, Grace was invited to the wedding. Once people learned that she had made this beautiful dress, she was set upon by all sorts of people. They too had trouble coming up with the words to describe the beauty and the fit of the dress. As people started to leave, it seemed easy and natural to say to Grace, "Can I still pick you up for church next Sunday?"

"Why, Tom, I'd be happy to see you!"

And so it went. We saw more and more of each other until one day I said, "Grace, you know I love you, and I want you to be my wife. Will you marry me?"

Six months later, we were married and moved into the farmhouse with Pa. Of course, she made her own wedding dress that made her look gorgeous. It has been four long years since the broken engagement to Linda, and finally, I feel happy and complete.

I would like to tell you about our wedding. Our plan followed closely the plan that Mame and Rocky used for their wedding. There were only a few major differences. One, we got married in the Mount Pleasant Methodist Church instead of the Yorkville Methodist Church. Two, Grace's parents paid for the food. And three, there was no $100 wedding dress since Grace made her own.

The Wedding Night

We were plenty nervous. Neither of us had any experience. I crawled into bed first and awaited Grace's arrival. There were two candles lit on either side of the bed, so I could see Grace approaching the bed in a long, blue cotton nightgown. As she lay down, I moved over and put my arm around her, and she seemed to move a little closer. Finally, I got up the nerve to put my hand on her calf, and slowly I crept up her leg. Just as I got to her thigh, I felt her stiffen, and the screaming started.

The house was surrounded with people. Most of them were screaming, "Shivaree! Shivaree!"

"Son of a bitch" were the only words that came to my mind. People were banging on pots and pans. I could tell the horses and cows were getting spooked. I had heard of these things, but I, of course, had never experienced one. From what I remember, they expect the couple being shivareed to offer food and drinks. No way in hell I was going to do that. In the morning, I found one of our cows tied to the front door. The outhouse was tipped over. Our buggy was hung by four ropes to the big maple tree in front of the house. Pa simply said, "You shoulda offered them some food and drink."

CHAPTER TEN

Grace

TOM IS A wonderful man. He's honest, hardworking, caring, and attentive. I couldn't ask for a more wonderful man than Tom. We're living in the Foxwell farmhouse with Tom's pa, and I love Tom and I love my life.

Not sure how much you know about me. My great-grandparents came from Scotland, and we've been farmers for as long as anyone can remember. I grew up on a farm in Mt. Pleasant, Wisconsin. My Pa raises mainly potatoes and cabbage. Early on, I spent many days with a hoe in my hands. I know hard work, and I'm not afraid of it. But I must admit, when I saw the chance to become a seamstress, I took it and never looked back. I was taught by my mother and my mother's mother, each of whom is an expert in her own right. Without bragging too much, I've taken my profession a step beyond what they know. I know style, and I know what looks best on a woman.

If I have a flaw, it's that I'm sometimes judgmental, as I have been told. I don't quite understand that criticism; doesn't everybody know what's right and what's wrong? Why is it that some people have such a hard time seeing the difference? I've never been called on it, but I can be a bit feisty and maybe a little insecure.

The first year of our marriage was near perfect. It took me a little while to get used to Tom's pa. Tom says that he hasn't been the same since his wife died. Other than that, it was the best year of my life. The second year started out with a bang. Of course, Tom told me all about his engagement with Linda well before he proposed. I can't fault him on that. It was the summer of 1912, and there was an ice cream social at the school. I was looking forward to it. We were having a great time, and then Joe and Linda Maranger showed up. I saw Tom's face at their entrance; it turned every shade of red. I looked at Linda; she was stunning. How do I compete with that? Plus, I already knew she'd been to college. How do I compete? Tom assured me that all that was in the past, but how can it be? He was with her for many years; she was his first love. You never completely get over that, do you? Tom gives me no reason to complain. There's really nothing he does, or has done, that should give me pause. Yet every time he's looking off into the distance, I fear he's thinking about Linda. Every time he's gone longer than I think he should be, I wonder, *Is he with Linda?* I know this sounds crazy. It has no basis, in fact, yet I can't seem to shake it.

The ice cream social was three years ago. Tom and I now have two children, Tom Jr. and Joseph, who's named after my dad. Am I happy? Not like I was that first year. I still have lingering doubts, maybe crazy doubts. Now Tom's pa has passed. He never was the same after his wife passed. Tom has more quiet times; logically, I can make sense of that. His pa has just passed, and he's now solely responsible for our family and our farm. But it's not all about logic. I still have this dark side that feels he's thinking about Linda.

Of course, from time to time we bump into Joe and Linda. Yorkville is not a big place. Tom now treats them like any other couple. Me, it seems like I behave like a real dope when I see the two of them. The worst part is that even though Tom behaves toward me like the perfect husband, I think from time to time I take out my insecurities on him. I'm not sure how to escape these feelings.

JAMES R. VYVYAN SR.

BOOK TWO

Tom Foxwell Jr.

CHAPTER ONE

Tom Jr.

TODAY AT MCQUARRY'S General Store, I heard Mr. Villwock say that alcohol was illegal. Heck, I thought alcohol was always illegal—at least that's what our minister says. Let me tell you a little about myself. My brother Joe and I are both eight. I've heard people say that's weird. I don't know why. One person said that we were Irish twins. I don't know what that means, but it didn't sound good to me. Joe and I were born ten months apart; what's the big deal? We're kind of like twins. We look alike, talk alike, and are best friends. People say we're very handsome. Maybe we are, I don't know. We really don't have any other close friends; no other kids our age live nearby.

Ma makes most of our clothes, and she's a great cook. She usually makes bacon and eggs for breakfast. Dinner at noon is usually ham, fried chicken, or beef with potatoes and peas or green beans. Ma makes great desserts—apple dumplings are my favorite. Nearly everything we eat is grown right here on our farm. There's really only one dinner I don't like. I remember coming in one day, and there was a cow's tongue lying on the cutting board. "Ma, what's that for?"

"Dinner."

"Ma, I can't eat that!"

The tongue was about ten inches long and five inches wide and kind of rough and scaly. "You put enough mustard on it and you'll like it." I never did like it, but I ate it.

Joe and I spend our time working with Pa or playing. My brother and I both enjoy helping Pa; it makes us feel important. Once in a while, we get in trouble while playing. Ma is the one that punishes us; Pa never does.

I'd like to tell you about what happened last month. It was the first week in March, and Monday came with a heat wave. It had been a cold winter, with tons of snow. Joe and I would trade off helping Pa milk the cows and doing the morning chores. Today is my day to do the morning chores. First up is feeding the calves. One of them has never drunk from a pail, so I put two fingers in her mouth and lead her head down into the water, and as she sucks my fingers, she gets the idea about drinking from a pail. Next I feed the chickens and gather the eggs. The feeding part is easy; gathering the eggs is not. Some of the eggs are just sitting in the nest, no problem. The others have an old hen sitting on them. As I reach in for the eggs, more often than not, the hen will squawk and peck my hand. It hurts! The next part is feeding the geese. The geese just run wild around the farmyard. So I sprinkle some cracked corn for them. The pigs also get some cracked corn and, of course, water. Finally, the sheep get some grain and water. When I'm done, I go back to the barn to see if Joe is done with his part of the milking. We change into our school clothes and walk the mile to school.

As Joe and I walk the mile to school, the snow is melting fast. We attend Yorkville School, the same school that Pa attended when he was a boy. Yorkville School is a one-room school with a wood-burning stove in the front corner. We won't be using the stove today. School is boring as usual. As we walk home, we can hardly believe how much snow has disappeared.

When we woke up on Tuesday, the first thing we heard was, "Son of a bitch!" We jumped out of bed and looked for Pa. We found him on the basement stairs, and the basement was four feet deep in water.

"Pa, what happened?"

"Well, you know the drain tile that goes from our basement to the canal?"

"Sure."

"Apparently, the canal has gone over its banks and forced the water up the tile and into our basement."

"What are we going to do?"

"Nothing we can do, everything we had in the basement is ruined."

I thought about what was in the basement. We had some tools, clothes, potatoes, apples, and jars of canned goods. Surely Ma's canned things would be okay. We walked out to the barn, and across from the house was a lake! Yesterday it had been a field like any other field; today it's a lake.

"There'll be no school today. I'll need your help."

After chores, the three of us spent time wading into the basement water trying to save as much as possible. Pa did pretty well, but for Joe and I, the water came up to our shoulders. Plus, the water was cold and yucky. What a terrible job. We did save some of the canned goods, tools, and clothing.

We spent that day, plus the rest of the week, home from school. Word got around that nearly all the roads were impassable. Not to worry; Pa had lots of things for us to do. Pa told us since spring appeared to be here, it was time to shear the sheep. They had a heavy coat from our cold winter.

Pa did most of the shearing. Joe and I would take turns putting the wool into burlap bags and helping hold the sheep being shorn. Later, we planned to sell the wool in Union Grove. When Pa's hands would start to cramp up from squeezing the shear, Joe and I would take turns at it. We were slow and clumsy, but we made some progress. When Pa's hands felt better, he would again take over, and we'd go back to bagging and holding the sheep. Sometimes we'd just take a break, and Pa usually had a piece of candy for us and, if we were lucky, a story about the old days. I know he loved us, and we loved him.

The second job was to castrate the hogs. I'd never done this before. Pa said we were old enough to do the job. I wasn't so sure. First, Joe and I would catch one of the fifteen-pound pigs. Of course, the cussed animals were deep in the mud. Then I would hold the pig upside down by his hind legs. At this point, the pig was squealing like a stuck pig. I know that sounds funny, but it's true. Pa took the razor blade and made a two-inch cut over each testicle. Then, he took his index finger and popped out each testicle. At this point, I winced and thought I could feel a pain in my crotch. He then snipped off the testicle, and Joe would dab the cut with some iodine. I thought Pa would sew up the wound, but no. We just let the pig go and caught the next one. You'd think the pig would die of infection.

On Friday, the weather turned. As warm as it was, it was now frigid, and it came with a strong north wind. By Saturday morning, it was ten degrees, and that lake across from the house was now frozen solid. Joe and I wanted to try our hand at ice skating, but Pa had more work for us. After church on Sunday, we finally had some time for ourselves. The water in the canal had dropped like a stone, and therefore, the water in our basement was gone. The basement was an absolute mess, but we wouldn't take on a job like that on a Sunday.

Joe and I went exploring. We walked along the canal, and we could easily see how high the water had been. As we walked farther, we found the spot where the water had washed out a hole in the bank of the canal and flooded the field. We found that we could walk through this hole and be under the ice!

If there was one difference between Joe and me, it was that Joe never seemed to know fear. When I looked at the hole leading under the ice, all I could think of was a wolf or a fox cornering us under there. I could tell that Joe saw nothing but an adventure. "Come on, Tom, let's explore!" And away we went.

Now here's the part I'll never forget. What had been a large lake, four feet deep, was now four inches of ice over nothing. The ice was supported by the canal bank on one side and some small hills on the other three sides. Once we were in, it felt like we were in another world, a world of our own. As we walked along under the ice, it was so weird and just a little spooky. A little light filtered through the ice. Joe found a stick and gave a poke at something stuck in the ice above. We heard a crack and then another crack and a third and finally a crash. The whole damn roof of ice fell on us. I heard Joe scream. I was knocked down but was able to get back up. "Joe! Joe!" No response. Then I saw his leg sticking out from under a huge chunk of ice. "Pa! Pa!" I yelled continually as I ran back to the house.

CHAPTER TWO

The Aftermath

A S MY HUSBAND laid Joe on the kitchen table, I remained calm on the outside, but on the inside, I was a mess. I put on a strong face, but beneath that I was jelly. I quickly saw Joe's chest rise and fall, and the jelly turned to anger. I put hot compresses on his forehead, and within five minutes, he came to with "What happened?"

Long ago, I'd gotten over the whole Linda mess. But during those times, I treated my husband and children with an attitude that was much less than they deserved. They had done nothing wrong. Now I find it a hard habit to break. I continue to treat them with a hard edge. I know I have trouble treating them with the love and kindness they deserve, but this time they have gone too far. My husband is a good man and the boys are good children, but now their weaknesses need to be dealt with. My husband just wants to play and laugh with the kids, and the kids take advantage of his lack of discipline.

"Okay, I want to know what happened, and I want to know now!"

Grace became quiet and Tom Jr. spoke.

I knew Joe was in no shape to reply, so I stammered as I began, "We, we were out exploring the canal, and we discovered the hole in the canal bank that caused our field to flood. So we kind of just took a step or two under the ice, and the whole thing fell in on us." I left out the part about Joe poking the ice with a stick, and I knew that Pa understood we went a whole lot farther than a step or two.

"You see, Tom, you haven't taught these boys any common sense. Any damn fool knows you don't go under a sheet of ice!"

"Now, Grace, they were just doing a little exploring."

"You don't get it, Tom, do you? These boys could have been killed, and it's because you don't discipline them. I want you to take a switch to both of these boys, and if you won't, I will."

"Please, Grace, just be thankful that they're okay, and I'm sure they will learn from this."

"They'll learn a whole lot more if you take a switch to them."

"You boys go to your room, and your ma and I will talk it over."

We left for our room, and Joe seemed quiet but okay. We tried to listen to what was going on below, but we couldn't hear much. Eventually we were called back down to the kitchen. Ma began, "We've decided that since you are so all fired interested in that canal, we have a job for you. You know that wet spot in the field by your uncle Walt's?"

"Yes, Ma."

"We want you to dig a trench, put in tile, and drain that spot."

Joe said, "But, Ma, we aren't even ten years old. We don't know nothing about putting in tile."

I added, "We're not strong enough or big enough to do a job like that. We'd need to dig a trench a hundred feet long and three feet deep!"

"It's your choice, the tile or twenty lashes with a switch."

"Yes, Ma."

"And, Tom, I don't want you helping those boys."

As you recall, this all happened on Sunday, and the digging was scheduled for the following weekend. By Saturday, Joe was back to his usual self, and thankfully the weather was sunny and warm. Things had been mighty quiet all week. Ma and Pa weren't talking to each other, and very little was being spoken to us. Early Saturday morning, we walked toward the wet spot; I had a shovel, and Joe had a spade. Pa had run a string from the wet spot to the canal showing us where to dig. We dug all Saturday morning, and we had a trench about ten inches deep across the entire hundred feet. If there was anything good about this job, it was the fact that the soil was fairly soft and didn't have many roots.

A little before noon, Pa brought out the clay tile on a wagon and also brought a little lunch and some lemonade.

"How you boys doing?"

Joe replied, "Okay, I guess, but my hands are getting sore."

"I thought about that, so I brought you boys some gloves."

"Thanks, Pa."

With that, Pa turned the wagon around and headed back to the barn.

By three, we were nearly dead, but we had managed to get the trench to about sixteen inches deep.

"Joe, I don't think we can do this."

"I know, Tom, but I don't know what else we can do but keep digging."

By chore time, Pa came out and picked us up with the wagon. He didn't say much, but we enjoyed hearing, "You boys got a real good start."

Sunday we were really surprised when, after chores and breakfast, Ma said, "You boys best be heading back to the tiling job."

I gasped, "On Sunday, what about church?"

"The good Lord will understand, plus remember, 'The Lord helps those who help themselves.'"

We looked at Pa, but he just kept his head down. So off we went.

We were two sad-looking boys. We were sore and tired.

"Joe, I don't think we can do this."

"I feel the same."

I know I had a couple of blisters, and I think Joe did too. As we approached the trench, something looked different.

"I can't believe it!" Joe exclaimed.

"Me neither."

Someone, or some people, had finished digging the trench! All we had to do was lay the tiles end to end and cover them up. This was still no small task for boys our age but doable.

At noon, Pa appeared with some sandwiches and lemonade. We didn't say anything about the miracle and neither did he. He just said, "You boys are making good progress." He turned the team around and headed home. Come about three, we finished and headed home, just in time for chores. As we came in for supper, we were met at the door by Ma.

"You boys finish your job?"

"Yes, Ma," we said in unison.

"Did you learn your lesson?"

"Yes, Ma."

"Good, let's not let this kind of thing happen again."

Joe and I knew enough to keep our heads down and our mouths shut.

CHAPTER THREE

Not Working

I'M AFRAID I'VE been giving you the wrong idea about our lives. We do more than work. Yes, we spend most of our time working, but there is far more to our lives than work.

For one, we spend time with family. My uncles Walt and Ben often come to family dinners with their wives and children. Their children are quite a bit older than Joe and me. Aunt Mame and her husband, Rocky, often attend, but they don't have children. Seldom does a month go by without several such meals. Ma is such a great cook that these meals usually happen at our house. The conversation is enjoyed by all. Will Rogers stories and quotes are a big favorite. One of my favorites is "After eating an entire bull, a mountain lion felt so good he started roaring. He kept it up until a hunter came along and shot him. The moral: When you're full of bull, keep your mouth shut." I've learned that there are many times when keeping your mouth shut is the best option.

Sundays are usually spent at church. Service is from 10:00–11:00 a.m. Often, there is a potluck meal following, and I really enjoy sampling the different hot dishes. It always amazes me that there is such variety in the food. Since there is no planning, you'd think that there might be a meal of all desserts, but that never happens. Occasionally the youth group, Ladies Aid, or Men's Club will put on a show. The show might be simply entertainment, or it might teach a lesson, based on scripture of course.

Joe and I like to play checkers. I usually beat Joe; he likes to take too many chances. Last Christmas, we got a Chinese checkers game. This is a game played on a six-pointed star. Your marbles start in one of the points, and by moving space by space or by jumping, you try to move your marbles from one point to the opposite point of the star. Occasionally, Ma or Pa will take us on in a game of Chinese checkers.

Ma is far better at these games than you might expect. She can be a formidable opponent.

Thinking about Ma, you might be surprised to know she loves to play cards. Last winter, she slipped and fell on the ice, breaking her kneecap. The doc said she should stay off her feet for a few weeks. I was surprised when Pa hired a servant girl named Jeanette to help out. Joe and I were told to keep Ma entertained. It turned out Ma wanted to play canasta. I didn't know she played cards. It turned out she really knew the game. Joe and I played canasta with her for weeks. I was surprised that she laughed and joked with us. I'd never seen that side of her.

Sometimes Joe and I would work on a project together. Once we took a wooden crate and tried to make it into a boat. We took pieces of wood and tried to plug all the holes in the crate. We launched it in the canal, but no matter how hard we tried, it kept leaking. We used a wide board as a paddle. Once, I sunk right in the middle of the creek, and Joe had to call Pa to rescue me. Pa has teased me about this a number of times since. Let me explain. The water was low; there was no danger of drowning, and there was almost no current. Somehow, though, I felt totally safe inside my sunken boat and really scared to leave it.

On cold winter nights, we like to listen to records. We have a Victrola that used to belong to Ma's parents. We only have a few records, maybe ten at the most. We have Al Jolson, Sophie Tucker, Eddie Cantor, and I forget the name of the singer but I love the song "Bye Bye Blackbird." If you're not familiar with a Victrola, you have to put a needle in the arm, crank it up, and you should be able to play a whole record at seventy-eight revolutions per minute before it needs cranking again.

I enjoy listening to these records and wish we had more. I also like the look of the nameplate on the Victrola, with the dog looking into the horn.

We also like to read. Joe likes books about the old west. I, on the other hand, like science fiction books. I especially like books about Mars. Some of the books I've read are *Gods of Mars*, *Princess of Mars*, and *Warlord of Mars*. You probably wonder where we get these books. Mr. McQuarry at the general store has an arrangement where, once a month, about twenty books are delivered and the previous books are sent back to the library in Racine. I've never been to a library.

If the weather is nice, we like to ride our horses: Pepper and Ranger. If we have the time and the money, we'll ride into Union Grove and have a soda at the drugstore. We might also ride over to Uncle Walt's or Uncle Ben's. Or we might also just go exploring. If there's a church or family picnic, we might get a bunch of us together and have a horse race. Joe's horse, Pepper, is just a little faster than mine, and he often wins the races.

So as you can see, our lives are far more than working.

JAMES R. VYVYAN SR.

CHAPTER FOUR

A Dark Day

ALTHOUGH IT HAPPENED six months ago, I remember this day like it was yesterday. It was a Friday, June 20, 1924. The day began miserably hot and humid. The three of us were soaked in sweat just finishing the daily chores. We were harnessing the horses to bring our hay in from the field, when Joe saw it first. He exclaimed, "Look!" As he pointed to the southwest, Joe, Pa, and I saw the darkest cloud we had ever seen. Black as ink, jet black, neither of these would do it justice. As we watched, we could tell it was coming fast. Pa spoke first, "I'll unhitch the horses. You try to get the chickens in the chicken house."

As we worked, we kept one eye on the clouds. They just kept getting closer and blacker, if that was possible. Just then, it looked like something was happening to the clouds farthest to our right. We could see multiple lightning strikes, and the thunder made our chests vibrate. Then Pa yelled, "Cyclone! Cyclone! Head for the basement." All three of us ran as fast as we could to the house. Pa yelled to Ma, "Cyclone! You and Jeanette get to the basement." We gathered in a corner far from any basement windows. Pa held me in his arms, and Ma held Joe. Jeanette was between Ma and Pa, and we were all sitting on the basement floor.

We couldn't see much. We were far from the windows, and of course, it was pitch-black outside. I asked Pa, "Have you ever seen anything like this before?" He just shook his head no. Then we heard it. People since have told me that cyclones sound like a freight train. I've never heard a freight train, so I don't know about that. What I heard was a tremendous wind and the house creaking and groaning, and then the sounds doubled and tripled. We looked up toward the basement joists, and we saw the whole house move on the foundation. Just so you know, our house is pretty big. It has five bedrooms, living room, parlor, etc. sitting on stone walls that are three feet thick. Yet the whole house moved about six inches on the foundation!

"Jesus Christ!" Pa didn't usually talk like that, and then he said, "Let us pray. Dear God, your humble servants beg of you to save us from this storm. Amen."

As fast as the wind had arrived, it left at the same speed. It was quiet—dead quiet. Nobody said a word. I thought to myself, *Now what do we do?* We waited about five minutes in absolute quiet, and then Joe sounded excited as he said, "Let's go look!" And so we did.

How to describe what we saw, I don't know where to start. Every farm building was gone except the chicken house. The barn gone, the windmill gone, the granary gone.

Pieces of these buildings lay scattered across the yard. Words failed me. We checked out the house, and yes, it had moved six inches, but since it was sitting on three-foot-thick walls, we thought it would be okay. Within fifteen minutes, neighbors started arriving. Uncle Walt and Uncle Ben were there first. It was strange; nobody said anything. They just looked around, stunned. Once in a while, you'd hear, "Holy shit!"

Then we started to think about our animals. Our horses were in the first floor of the barn, and as you can see from the picture, it was still intact. The horses were fine. What about the cows? They had been

JAMES R. VYVYAN SR.

out to pasture; there wasn't time to get them in the barn. Of the twenty cows, we could find only thirteen of them. The pigs were in a building that was completely destroyed. Yet we found the fifteen pigs seemingly healthy, running around in the debris. Of the ten sheep, we found eight of them crushed in the wreckage. The chicken house survived, so the chickens were in good shape.

The first day was spent simply in awe of the power of the storm. The next day, we started to think, now what? Luckily, or smartly, Pa had insurance with Yorkville Mutual Insurance, and it appeared that they would pay for the rebuilding.

Think about our condition. The windmill was down, so we rigged up a hand pump to get water for ourselves and animals. The crops were funny. One field would be completely destroyed and the next untouched. The hay that we were about to harvest that day had just disappeared. Many of our fields were blanketed with boards, papers, shingles, etc. Most of it was ours, but some of it was not. There must be other places like ours that have been destroyed.

The people. The people that stopped by were of two types. About half showed their concern and offered to help clean up the mess. The other half just wanted to gawk. So as our family was working as hard as we could along with many neighbors, others were just standing around. We were all more than a little put out by them. Plus, it seemed very important to one of them to tell us how it wasn't a cyclone but a tornado. We didn't find that very helpful.

As time went on, many stories came out of this cyclone—not just from our farm but from the other farms that were hit too. Some of these stories are true and others well . . . here are the stories I can vouch for:

1. There was a straw going through a fence post. Most people, when they hear this, visualize an eight-inch round fence post with a straw going through the center. Not the case. I saw a straw going through the side of the fence post, maybe at most two inches through the wood.
2. Our cupola was found three miles away in Ives Grove. The cupola sat on top of the barn roof and probably weighed two hundred pounds. Wow!
3. Our buggy had been sitting in the barnyard. After the cyclone, we found it on top of the first floor of the barn.

4. The remaining seven cows were found alive three miles to the north. Did they fly there or walk there?

Now, for the other stories going around, I'll let you be the judge of whether they are true or false.

1. A woman near Union Grove claimed that the cyclone tore her baby from her arms, and the baby was found unharmed in the yard.
2. Vanswols claimed that their chicken house was picked up, carried fifty feet, and set down with the chickens still on their nests.
3. The Vivians found one of their horses ten feet high in an old oak tree.

How do we look at this now that it's over? We thank God that we're alive. We thank God that our beautiful house survived. We thank God that he heard our prayers. Most of all, we simply hope that we will never have to go through something like this again.

CHAPTER FIVE

The Silo

A S THE FATHER of Tom Jr. and Joe, I've failed miserably. I have to tell someone about what happened and what's going on inside of me. My wife doesn't want to talk about it. My brothers and sister care, but apparently, they think it's too painful to bring it up. I've got to tell someone or I'll bust.

It all happened about three months ago, and to understand my story, you need to understand what a silo is and how it's used on the farm. A silo is a cement cylinder somewhat like a Quaker Oats box. Ours has no roof, but many of them have either a cement or metal roof. The fact that ours has no roof is important to the story. Our silo is forty feet tall and fourteen feet across, and in the fall, we fill it with chopped corn. We chop the whole plant: stalk, tassel, and cob. The corn is sealed in the silo, somewhat like a fruit jar so it doesn't spoil, and we feed it to the cows all winter long. We refer to this feed as silage.

The first tool needed to fill a silo is a corn binder, which cuts the cornstalks and ties about ten stalks into a bundle. These bundles are loaded onto a wagon and taken to the silo. The second machine, often called a silo filler, is set up at the silo, and it cuts the corn into three-fourths-inch pieces and blows these pieces up an eight-inch pipe and into the top of the silo. This machine needs to be powered by a tractor. We have a corn binder, but we don't have a silo filler or a tractor. So we work with our neighbor Bob Moyle. He has a tractor and a silo filler, and we have a corn binder.

To fully understand my story, you have to understand the situation I'm in. My wife has grown accustomed to having hired help. We've all come to love Jeanette, and we think of her as part of the family. I want my wife to be happy, but it costs. I'd love to have a tractor and a car and maybe have a hired man to help me out. All these things cost. Plus, we still have a substantial mortgage on the farm. What is a farmer to do? The only thing I can do is to grow more corn, oats, wheat, and hay and produce more milk. We've tiled all the wet spots on the farm, so we are now producing on every acre of our farm. I've even rented a few extra acres from the widow Benson. With these extra acres, I thought we could handle a few more cows. The problem with a few more cows is that we would run out of silage before spring pasture is available. What to do? I came up with what I thought was a great idea. Usually we would fill the silo about two feet from the top. What if we not only filled it to the top but also continued blowing silage up and put a rounded top of silage on the silo? Think of a huge scoop of ice cream on top of an ice cream cone. We would certainly have enough silage to feed a few more cows.

The day we put the rounded top on the silo was a Saturday. Bob Moyle had the shingles and wasn't available to help. So it was the three of us: Tom, Joe, and me. The silo was nearly full, and all we had to do was put the rounded top on it. We first went to the cornfield and loaded up a big load of bundled corn. The boys had a tough time loading a bundle, but they worked together. As the wagon was piled higher I did most of the lifting, and Tom and Joe would take turns driving the team and helping me with the bundles. When the wagon was full, we pulled up to the silo filler. It normally took two people to feed the bundles into the silo filler, and this time we needed a third to climb to the top of the silo and fork the silage around to form the cone on top of the silo. Joe volunteered.

The plan was, when Joe had no more room for silage, he would throw some silage down on top of Tom and me, signaling us to stop. I started up Moyle's McCormick-Deering 10-20, and we began filling the silo. This all worked according to plan. After a time, Joe threw some silage down, and we stopped. Tom and I drove what was left on the wagon out to the pasture for the cows to eat. When we got back, I expected Joe to have climbed down and be waiting for us. No Joe. I found him lying at the bottom of the silo.

What the hell happened? I pictured Joe climbing down from the mound of silage. I guess I hadn't thought through how difficult it would be to climb down. In the last few months, I've replayed the scene a million times. The steps would be partially hidden by the mound of corn silage. Plus, you know Joe never did know fear. It boils down to one thing: it's all my fault. How do I deal with causing something like this? I've always been able to accept the mistakes of others, but this is my mistake. That makes all the difference. It haunts me every waking minute and nighttime too. Still the family has to eat. I still have to milk the cows. I feel the Black Dog coming back to me with a vengeance. Perhaps the worst of it is thinking about how Tom Jr. will handle this.

CHAPTER SIX

Jake

I WANT TO tell you about my friend Jake. Jake is nine like me but just a little smaller with brown hair. Jake is a good friend. He never argues with me and pretty much agrees with me about everything. Ma and Pa don't seem to like Jake.

Jake helps me a lot. Occasionally, he will help me with the morning chores, but more often, he'll help me with the evening chores. I'm just a little bit stronger than he is. When it comes to carrying the empty milk cans to the barn, he really struggles. He's also really bad at gathering the eggs, and he has a terrible fear of the hens pecking him.

We go on lots of adventures. When we're not working, we like to explore the canal. We like to catch the crayfish and minnows that live in the canal. Two months ago, we discovered some big fish coming up the canal. We ran back to the barn to get a pitchfork to spear them. Jake can't run as fast as I can. We didn't spear any of the fish, but we came real close. There seemed to be a problem between actual position of the fish and where it appeared to be as we looked through the water.

When the weather is bad, we like to listen to records on the Victrola. He likes the same records that I do. The only thing we ever disagree on is that he doesn't like to crank the Victrola.

Jake doesn't do much with our family. He doesn't go to church with us and has never attended any of our family picnics. It seems he only likes to do things with me.

I hear Ma calling us for supper. "Thomas Foxwell Jr., get yourself to the table!"

"Can Jake have supper with us?"

"Now that's enough of that nonsense, your brother has been dead for almost a year. There is no Jake."

CHAPTER SEVEN

First Look

HERE I AM at the age of thirteen, and I've never been outside of Racine County. That is about to change.

J. D. Beckett owns an Angus farm about three miles from home. Mr. Beckett is president of a Racine bank and operates a hundred-acre farm containing about fifty Black Angus cattle. Some would say it is a hobby farm; Mr. Beckett would not. Dad says an Angus farm in this part of Wisconsin is crazy. He says compare one Angus cow with one of our Holstein cows. Both cows require the same amount of feed and both produce one calf each year. The Holstein, however, also produces 15,000 pounds of milk. Which do you think is the better investment?

None of that really matters to my story. Mr. Beckett has a hired man, Jim, who lives on the place and raises the crops and takes care of the cattle. Jim is a hard worker and knows a lot about farming, but I've never much cared for him. I can't quite put my finger on why. Jim doesn't know much about showing beef cattle. I, on the other hand, have been showing Angus cattle for the last three years at the county fair and, if I say so myself, know quite a bit about showing beef cattle. I've learned by observing, showing cattle, and reading. Our local 4-H club has provided a number of brochures on beef cattle. I've read them all a hundred times. My knowledge of beef cattle is how I got involved with Mr. Beckett.

All of Mr. Beckett's cattle are registered Angus. The cattle are registered by the American Angus Association. This means that Mr. Beckett must be able to prove the ancestors of each cow were registered and have each animal graded and tattooed with a unique ID number. That's where I come in. Beckett's hired man, Jim, needed help to catch and hold the young cattle so that a tattoo could be put in the ear of each calf. Also, as adults, the cows are graded by an employee of the

American Angus Association. Each cow receives a grade from 1 to 100, where 100 is perfect. I doubt any cow has ever received a grade of 100.

Jim also needed help grooming the cows so that they would get the highest grade possible. So I washed each cow and gave them a haircut. It's a really special haircut designed to hide their flaws and accentuate their strong points. For example, a nice straight back is a plus, so I would trim the top line of each cow hiding any dips or bumps. Also, I would clean their hooves and polish them with black shoe polish. There are a few things that border on cheating. I'll just mention one. White hair on a Black Angus is frowned upon. Some people put on black shoe polish to hide any white hair. There are many other tricks that are marginal or illegal; I know most of them, but I would never use them.

Not to brag, but I can tell a quality animal when I see one. One of the cows is obviously superior to the others. Her name is Windsong Esther of Aberdeen; we just call her Esther.

Just as I was finishing the grooming, the grader arrived. I paraded each animal in front of him. He, meanwhile, compared each cow against the ideal Angus cow. Included in the grading was how the animal moved and walked. The first three cows graded in the 70s. The fourth cow graded 81. The last cow to be graded was Esther, and she graded a 94. This was outstanding and unheard of.

About a week later, Mr. Beckett stopped by our farm. "Mr. Foxwell, I'd like to borrow your son for a week. I believe I have the best Angus cow in the nation, and I intend to prove it. I want your son and my hired man to take Esther to the American Royal Livestock Exhibition in Kansas City."

"Whoa, that's a big trip, must be six hundred miles. How are you going to do that?"

"My hired man is outfitting our Model T truck with a trailer for Esther. I'm proposing my hired man and your son take Esther to the show in the trailer."

"Let me talk it over with my wife, and we'll let you know."

I didn't quite know how I felt about the trip. I liked the idea of seeing some of the country, but a week with Jim kind of scared me. Dad and Mom talked it over, and they agreed that if we weren't busy on the farm, I could go. I also found out that the show was in November; I'd be missing school. Yippee! Oh, one more thing, Beckett offered me

$100 for the week! That was four times the going rate for a thirteen-year-old. Wow!

It was a Wednesday in late October when Jim and I loaded the Model T truck with feed, grooming tools, and our personal belongings. We then carefully loaded Esther into the trailer and off we went. Our route would take us through Rockford, Illinois; Davenport, Iowa; and Des Moines, Iowa. I was beyond excited. I found that Jim didn't talk much, and mostly, we rode in silence. He was twice as big as I was with bulging muscles. (He still kind of scared me.) The size and flatness of the fields amazed me. I got a real kick out of seeing the farmers harvest their corn. Each farmer had a little different method, and of course, the equipment they used could be very different. Every four hours or so, we would stop for gas and food; of course, Esther needed food and a stretch of her legs too. One time we were almost out of gas, and we were forced to pay twenty cents a gallon for gas!

By the end of the first day, we made it to Davenport, Iowa. We found a hotel just outside of town, where Esther could do a little grazing on the back lawn. After supper, Jim asked, "I'm going to get a drink, care to come along?"

"No, I'm pretty tuckered out. I'm heading for bed."

I wasn't quite sure what Jim was asking. Was he asking me to have some alcohol with him? It was tempting, but if Mom found out, there would be hell to pay. Jim returned about midnight and reeked of alcohol. We only had one bed, and he climbed in next to me. In a short time, he was snoring like a small tornado.

The next day, we arrived at the Royal Exhibition and got Esther comfortable in her stall. As soon as Esther was comfortable, I took a look around at the competition. There appeared to be fourteen Angus cows in Esther's class. I looked each one over carefully, and there was only one that I thought might be better than Esther. This cow was from Lakeland Farms in South Dakota. She was being cared for by two young men in their early twenties. The judging was to take place on Saturday, so we had some time to spare.

Jim and I set out to see the sights in Kansas City. I had never seen so many people, nor have I ever seen what my parents called darkies. The buildings were so huge; I don't even know how many floors they had. Soon we came across a huge theater, Schubert's Missouri, and it was advertising someone named Al Jolson. Jim said this was a burlesque show that we couldn't miss. What a show; I'd never seen anything like it. Mr. Jolson could sing and dance better than anyone I'd ever seen or heard of. Plus the theater was so huge; I bet it had over two thousand seats! One thing I didn't expect is the bubblers had signs over them, Whites Only.

When we came out, there was a commotion in the streets. A group of people were marching down the street in bed sheets with hoods over their heads. I asked Jim, "Who are they?"

"Well, they are the Ku Klux Klan, and they stand for Protestantism, morality, and patriotism."

"That sounds pretty good, so why do they have their faces covered?"

Jim didn't reply. The next day, I picked up a paper and found out that hatred against Negros, Catholics, and Jews was a better description of what they stood for. The hoods made a lot more sense now. I was proud of our nation's supreme court because the paper said the Supreme Court ruled the Ku Klux Klan was illegal in Kansas. I was beyond dead tired, but we had agreed that I would sleep next to Esther. We'd both heard stories about dirty tricks being pulled at these competitions.

The next day, Friday, was wide open. I rose early and fed, watered, and exercised Esther. Jim arrived about ten and appeared a little worse for the wear, if you know what I mean. Jim looked at the posted schedule and told me that at 1:00 p.m. was listed Vocational Agricultural Judging. "What's that?"

Jim said this is where high school boys, enrolled in agriculture, try to judge beef cattle. I thought to myself, *I'll probably never go to high school.*

Then Jim said, "Why don't you enter?"

"I'm not in high school."

"Who'd know?"

"Well, I don't know. I might get in trouble."

"Suit yourself."

I thought about it for a while. Who would know? I'd kind of like to test my knowledge of beef cattle against these high school boys. So I surprised even me; I entered the contest and put down that I was a student at Union Grove High School!

At 1:00 p.m., the contest started, and four beef steers were paraded in front of about fifty boys. Each steer had a number, and each boy was to put on paper the order of these steers from best to worst. The simplest way to explain judging beef steers is that a perfect steer should look like a big rectangular block on four straight legs. Special attention should be paid to the hind quarters (the butt) because that's where the steaks come from. Then a second group of four was brought out and then a third. The results were handed to the official and would be compared to the professional judge who just happened to be from the University of Wisconsin. The results were to be announced tomorrow morning before the beef cow competition.

By now, it was 3:00 p.m., and Jim had an idea. "I found out that *The Jazz Singer* is playing at the Electric Theater. We absolutely have to go."

"What's *The Jazz Singer*?"

"It's a movie and not just any movie. This is the first movie that people actually speak. Every movie I've ever seen has been a silent film, not this one!"

"I've never seen any movie."

"Get a move on, we're going."

I don't have words to explain how great this movie was. I was surprised that Al Jolson was in this movie too, and he sang five or six songs. The movie was fantastic!

Jim dropped me off at the cow barn about 7:00 p.m., and I decided to take another look at the competition. A surprise awaited me. The excellent cow from Lakeland Farms didn't look so good. I've seen this at our county fair. Sometimes it's all the excitement or the people or different-tasting water. This cow was definitely off her feed, meaning she wasn't eating or drinking and probably hadn't for the last three or four days. I tucked myself in next to Esther and was a little more confident that Esther would win tomorrow.

It was sometime after midnight that I heard something. I quietly got up, and the barn was almost perfectly still. There wasn't much light but enough to make out a little. First thing I noticed was the cow from Lakeland was out of her stall. I walked outside, and I could make out a cow in the grooming area. As I got a little closer, I could see it was the Lakeland cow and one of the two Lakeland boys was working on her. He had a garden hose inserted down her throat and connected to a five gallon pail. He was pumping her full of something, I didn't know what. Just then a hand, like a vise, grabbed my arm.

"You better forget what you've seen here if you know what's good for you!"

Before I could say a word, Jim appeared out of nowhere, and he had the boy in a choke hold. "You let go of that boy or you're dead meat!"

The boy's grip fell away from my arm. "Jim, they're pumping that cow full of something, that's not legal!"

"I know."

Jim stayed the night with me and Esther, and as soon as the administration building opened, I was there with the story of what happened. The administrator, a man named Lamping, heard my story. "We'll have to have a hearing, and we need to do it quick. The judging starts in four hours. Be here at nine thirty." I went back and told Jim, and he assured me that he'd come along too.

At nine thirty, it was Jim, me, the two Lakeland boys, and Mr. Lamping. "Okay, Mr. Foxwell, go ahead and tell us what you saw."

I told the story of what I had seen and how I had been threatened.

"Okay, now let's hear the other side."

The bigger of the two Lakeland boys started to speak. "That boy is telling one big lie, he just wants us to get disqualified so he can win the competition." The other Lakeland boy nodded in agreement.

"Since it's one man's word against the other, I'm going to have to remain neutral, but I'll be watching each of you closely," Lamping said.

As we left, I told Jim over and over how unfair it was. They were cheating. Jim just nodded, but then he said, "If we win, we know we'll have done it honestly and we'll know that Esther is the best cow here. If they win, they'll never know if their cow won because it was the best or because they cheated." With that, I got to work doing the final washing, grooming, and fitting of Esther.

At noon an announcement was made to gather in the arena for the revealing of the winner of Vocational Agricultural Judging Contest. Jim and I stood together as the announcement was made.

"In third place from Alexandria, Virginia, Robert Hooks. Robert had only two errors in his placing. Congratulations, Robert! In second place from Grand Forks, North Dakota, William Kind. William had only one animal out of position in his placing. Congratulations, William! In first place, with every animal in its correct position is Tom Foxwell Jr. from Union Grove, Wisconsin. Come up and get your trophy, Tom!"

What to do? I've won a trophy in a contest that I wasn't eligible to enter. Jim gave me a shove. I walked forward, accepted the trophy, and shook the hand of the presenter. My stomach was doing cartwheels. I can't accept this, or can I? I thought for a moment and headed straight to the administration building. "Mr. Lamping, I've got to talk to you. I'm in a hell of a fix. Everything I told you this morning was absolutely true, but I lied when I entered the judging contest. I'm not in high school and, therefore, not eligible to enter. I want to return the trophy."

"Son, I knew you were telling the truth this morning. I wish I could have ruled in your favor. I think even more of you now for being so honest about the contest. Nobody deserves this trophy more than you. Take it, enjoy it, and be proud of who you are and what you have accomplished."

The judging was about to start. I pinned Esther's number to my shirt and slowly led Esther into the ring with the other thirteen cows. One of the keys to showing an animal is to always keep one eye on the judge. After all, he is the only person that matters. A second key is to keep your animal's four legs squarely underneath her, just like the legs of a table. The fourteen cows slowly paraded around the ring with the judge in the center. Then the judge motioned us to line up the cows in a straight line. The judge came around and felt the muscling of each of the cows, then also spoke to each of us. He asked me, "How old is your animal?" Luckily, I knew precisely how old Esther was. The judge then picked out four animals to parade around the ring. I assumed that meant we were the top four. Of course, besides Esther, the Lakeland cow was there too. The boy leading the Lakeland cow glared at me from time to time, and once when the judge wasn't looking, he gave Esther a poke, hoping she would break out of position. It didn't work. I'd spent a lot of time getting Esther to lead properly and behave under all circumstances.

Two of the four were sent back to stand with the bottom ten. It was just Esther and the Lakeland cow. The judge began to speak. "These are the two finest Angus cows I have ever seen. You could look long and hard to find a fault with either one. In fact, if we had two trained, professional judges here, they might pick different animals to be the winner, it's that close. But I have to pick a winner, and I choose . . ." and he went over and slapped the Lakeland cow.

Jim came over and consoled me. In fact, a dozen or more strangers came over and consoled me. Each of them saying that they thought I was robbed. It hurt, I wanted so bad to beat those cheaters.

In the morning, I woke up feeling better. I have a trophy and an obvious talent for judging cattle. That's going to come in handy for a farmer. Plus, Mr. Beckett has the second best Angus cow in the nation. That's going to help his reputation and the reputation of his farm.

The ride home was long and boring. I had a lot of time to think about the burlesque house, the talkie, Esther, the Lakeland boys, and Jim. The last two were a bit of a problem for me. The Lakeland boys I could forgive, kind of. Maybe they didn't know any better, but more likely, they were just snakes. Now Jim, that's another story. He saved me when I needed him. He took me to some great shows. But the things he said about the Ku Klux Klan, that I can't forgive or forget.

CHAPTER EIGHT

Graduation

TONIGHT, MAY 18, 1928, I graduated from eighth grade! I've had a good year, and I feel strong. I think I can do more work in a day than most men I know. Last week, my teacher, Ms. Lewis, came to me and suggested that I go to high school. I was surprised; nobody in our family has ever gone to high school. She indicated that I was the smartest student in my class and that I could do more arithmetic in my head than most of my fellow students could do on paper. Of course, I was flattered, but why would I want to go to high school? I've always wanted to be a farmer, and Pa needs me. Still, several of my friends would be going to high school—Mack Moyle, Bill Shepherd, and Tom Skewes, to name a few.

My time at Yorkville School has been mostly good. I don't really enjoy the schoolwork, but still I've had some good times. I've been involved in a few pranks. I'm pretty shy around girls, but that didn't stop me from locking Mary Moyle in the outhouse. Another time, we had a new student, and I was able to switch the Boys and Girls signs on the outhouses, which led to some interesting times. I could go on, but you get the idea.

On the other hand, I've been embarrassed a few times. The last two years, I've ridden my horse, Pepper, to school. I am pretty proud of Pepper, and I know I sit extra tall in the saddle when I know someone is watching. Well, one day, I stopped to get Ma some bread at McQuarry's store. I then rode home past the school at a nice trot, sitting extra tall in the saddle. Several students pointed and smiled, and I was oh-so proud and sat even taller. When I got home, I realized that at each bounce another slice or two of bread had fallen out, and I only had a few slices left.

Another such time came on Spring Cleanup Day. Every May we have a day where we do a thorough cleaning of the school and the grounds. This would include dusting, cleaning the windows, mopping the floors, raking the four acres of grass, and picking up branches that have fallen over winter. I was working outside on the grass and branches along with a few friends. By the time we were done, we had quite a pile of grass and branches. We got permission from Ms. Lewis to burn the pile. Only the pile was a little damp, and it wouldn't keep burning. I knew that Ms. Lewis had a gas can in the back of her 23 Ford. I knew I should have asked, but I thought, *I'll graduate in a couple weeks, what can she do?* I'd never worked with gas before; we don't have a car or a tractor. I got what I thought was a modest amount and threw it on the pile. There was a mighty roar and a blast that knocked me over. When I got up, Mack Moyle said, "Where are your eyebrows?" Just then Ms. Lewis came storming out of the school. Apparently, the blast had broken a window in the school. For the last two weeks, some of my classmates (I won't call them friends) have been calling me Boomer.

I probably should bring you up to date on Ma and Pa. After Joe died, Ma went a little nutty. She did some things that I'd be embarrassed to put on paper. However, she seems to be getting it back together. Pa, on the other hand, is stuck. He hasn't changed a thing since Joe died. He doesn't talk much and has lost his desire to work. Sure, he does what he has to do but no more. Something needs to change.

CHAPTER NINE

Farming

THE DAY AFTER graduation Pa and I talked. "Pa, you know I want to farm with you, but we've got to get bigger and more modern. We need more land, a tractor, and a combine."

"Tom, I don't know if we can afford it."

"We can't afford not to. All the other farmers are getting tractors and combines, and we'll be left behind. Plus, I've been thinking, if we got a tractor that could pull a two-bottom plow that would more than double the amount of land we can work. Plus, you don't have to take breaks with a tractor. We could keep the horses, and then we would triple our rate of plowing. And with the combine, the two of us could do the work of a dozen men with a threshing machine!"

"Who's going to do all this work? You know I don't have the will like I used to."

"Pa, you know I can do as much work as most any man, and I promise you'll be happy with me as a partner."

"Let me talk to your mother."

So that's how it went. We purchased a Fordson tractor, Minneapolis combine, and Pa even got a used car. Most of what I said turned out to be true, with a few exceptions. The Fordson tractor could only pull a one-bottom plow and was a real beast to start in cold weather. In fact, when it was real cold, we would just use the horses. The combine did cut down on the labor, but it didn't have the capacity that the old forty-inch threshing machine did.

The car really surprised me. There were only a few of us still going to church in a buggy. So I guess I shouldn't be too surprised, but Pa bought a Buick! He could have purchased a brand-new Ford for under $400, but he paid more than that for a three-year-old Buick. There are a few things about Pa that I still haven't figured out.

The first year, we rented the rest of the widow Benson's farm and our harvest was great. What's more, the prices were good; they didn't call it the roaring twenties for nothing! The second year, we rented Villwock's farm and it was a lot of work, but we had another outstanding year. In fact, we were able to finish paying for the tractor, combine, and car. Pa also told me that he was able to pay off more of the original mortgage. He didn't tell me how much was left on the mortgage, and I didn't ask.

There were a couple of interesting things that happened during these two years. One is kind of funny, and the other not so much. The funny story I got from Ma: I wasn't there. Pa only had the Buick for about a month, and he was driving it into the garage. Apparently, he had a momentary lapse, and when he wanted the car to stop, he simply said, "Whoa!" When the car didn't stop he shouted, "*Whoa!*" The car killed as it hit the back wall of the garage.

The second story is a lot more serious. I was plowing the land over on Highway A. This land contains about a four-acre peat bog. If you're not familiar with a peat bog, it is soil that has a lot of plant matter and is usually quite loose and very wet. In fact, most years, we left about two acres of the four untilled. As I was plowing, each round I got closer and closer to the untilled area. Each round I thought, *Well, I can probably go one more round before I get stuck*. I said that to myself about six times, and on the seventh round, sure enough, I got stuck. The hitch of the tractor was resting on the ground, and the big rear wheels simply spun. I unhooked the plow, thinking that would be enough to free me. I was able to move about ten feet forward, but then I was stuck tighter than ever.

Now what am I going to do? I could walk the mile back to the farm and have Pa hitch up the horses, and maybe they could pull me out. Two problems with that idea—one, I don't think they could pull me out, and two, if they could pull me out, Pa would never let me forget that the horses saved me and the tractor. The second plan would be to walk a mile and a half over to Bob Moyle's and ask him to get the 10-20 tractor started and come over and pull me out. Two problems with this plan: one, I don't like to ask for help from neighbors, and two, I'm afraid that he would get stuck and we'd have a "mell of a hess!"

Then a third plan occurred to me. Here's the deal.

1. I was able to pull a six-foot wooden fence post out of the fence line.
2. I laid the post in front of the big rear wheels underneath the tractor, forming a right angle with the tractor frame.
3. I made sure that the post was between two lugs on both sides of the tractor.

My plan was to put the tractor in low gear and engage the clutch very slowly. The rear wheels will force the post down into the soil lifting the tractor out of the peat and propelling it forward. So I did just that, but when I let out the clutch instead of lifting the tractor out of the peat, the front end of the tractor rose and rose and rose, and before I knew it, the tractor flipped over backwards pinning me underneath the steering wheel.

I was momentarily stunned. When my head cleared, I knew I was hurt and had at least a couple of broken ribs. What's more, I'm pinned under the tractor and gas is dripping from the gas tank on top of me! Every breath hurt, and I thought my sixteen-year life might be over. When I calmed down, I thought about how soft and loose peat bogs were, and I began to dig with my hands. It took me close to an hour before I was able to dig myself out. Friends told me later that the Fordson tractor was known for flipping over backwards. In fact, one friend referred to the Fordson as the Widow Maker.

Now, as I look back, I realize if the ground had been any harder I'd be dead. If I hadn't unhooked the plow, I would have been crushed between the tractor and the plow. Farming is a dangerous way to make a living. But hey, we've had two good years, have some modern machinery, more land to work, and paid off a substantial amount on our mortgage. It's October 20, 1929, and the roaring twenties are coming to an end. I wonder what the thirties will bring.

JAMES R. VYVYAN SR.

CHAPTER TEN

The Depression

O N OCTOBER 29, 1929, the stock market crashed. We heard about it a few days later, but at first, we weren't too sure how it would affect us. There were stories going around about people jumping to their death. In fact, one story had the hotelkeepers asking guests, "Do you want a room to sleep in or jump from?" I'm not sure that's true, but that's what we heard.

We had already sold our grain for the year, but it soon became clear that farm prices were tanking. In fact, the grain we recently had been selling for over $2 per bushel was now 65 cents and falling! Milk prices were falling too, but at least it gave us some cash every week. But to be honest, the crash didn't affect us as badly as it did the city folks. We raise all our own meat, potatoes, and vegetables. We have our own milk to drink. Ma makes most of our clothes, some of them out of feed sacks. The amount of things that we purchase is really quite small. Salt, sugar, flour, shoes, gas, and seed are among the few things that we need to purchase. Some of our friends who work in Racine are much worse off. In fact, the *Racine Daily Journal* announced 25 percent unemployment and breadlines!

Life took a different turn for us on November 15, 1930. Pa was opening mail at the kitchen table, and I saw tears come to his eyes. "What's the matter, Pa?"

"Tom, the bank is foreclosing on us."

"*What!*"

"The bank is foreclosing on our farm."

"How much do we owe?"

"Well, our mortgage is $3,540, and at 2 percent, we owe $70.80, and we don't have it."

I was beyond shocked. I had no idea we still had a mortgage that large. I had no idea that we had missed the interest payment.

"Pa, why haven't you told me about this?"

"Tom, you've worked so hard. I just didn't have the heart to tell you, and frankly, I'm embarrassed. If I hadn't bought that fancy Buick, we could have paid the interest."

"Pa, I've got about twenty dollars in the bank, but we've got to meet with the president of the bank, Mr. Wilson."

The next day, Pa and I sat down with Mr. Wilson. Mr. Wilson started, "This is a very painful day for all of us. Yours will be the third farm I've foreclosed on this month. I've set an auction date for January 10."

I thought Pa was going to jump right through the ceiling. *"You did what?"*

"I've set an auction date for January 10."

Pa sat for a moment, and then he said, "Do you know what a penny auction is?"

Mr. Wilson's face turned red with anger. "We've never had one of those around here, and we never will!"

Pa replied, "Don't be too sure."

I knew what a penny auction was. All the local farmers gather at the farm being auctioned off, let's say Mr. Smith's farm. The auctioneer starts the bidding, "What do I hear for this fine farm of eighty-five acres, buildings and all?" One of the farmers responds, "Ten cents." The auctioneer goes on, "Come on, boys, don't be like that, what do I hear for this fine farm?" Another farmer responds, "I bid a quarter." The idea being to buy the farm for such a small amount that Mr. Smith can keep his farm. If anyone bids a reasonable amount, someone holds up a noose or pretends they have a gun in their pocket. Most people are too frightened to bid. It is an ugly thing.

I decided that I had to speak. "Mr. Wilson, I have twenty dollars that I can pay right now, and if you could just give us an extension of ninety days, I give you my word that we'll be able to pay the rest of the $75."

"Now, Tom, what makes you think that you can raise that kind of money?"

"I give you my word, sir. Have you ever heard of a Foxwell going back on his word?"

"Can't say that I have."

For the next ninety days, in fact, for the next three years, I had no personal life. All I did was work. I still did all the regular farmwork, and that was no small task. In addition, I worked at the local gas station, sold Christmas trees, and milked the neighbor's cows. Plus, I made it known that if something needed to be done, I'd do if for a fair price. My proudest day was when Pa and I went to the bank and paid off the loan. I couldn't help but say to Mr. Wilson, "I told you a Foxwell never goes back on his word."

Mr. Wilson simply said to Pa, "You've got a son to be mighty proud of."

I thought about those words for a long, long time. They felt mighty good. I never did get much praise around home. Maybe once in a while if I did an exceptional job of plowing or combining. It would be nice to hear praise for being a smart, honest, caring, loving son.

It dawned on me one day that I've been killing myself for a farm that wasn't even partially mine. I approached Pa. "I'm your only child, and I assume the farm will someday be mine. Couldn't we make a partnership agreement now? I've been working for next to no wages. I'd like to have a share of the profits and a say in how we do things."

"Your Ma and I have talked about it, and for now the answer is no."

For the next week or so, I could tell something was brewing. Ma and Pa weren't talking much, and I could feel a chill in the air. Finally, one morning it broke at the breakfast table.

"Damn it, woman, we've gone through hell, and we need a break. I want all of us to board the North Shore Train and go to the World's Fair in Chicago."

"You're crazy as a hoot owl, we don't have the money, and who's going to milk the cows and feed the animals?"

I was dumbfounded. In my entire life I had never heard Pa speak to Ma like that. Usually, what Ma wanted, Ma got and with no argument.

Pa continued, "Well, we're going, and I'll work out the details."

"I'll be damned if I'm going."

"So be it."

I have to admit I was excited. The idea of going to the World's Fair was beyond anything I'd ever dreamed of. Plus, I kind of like Pa standing up to Ma for a change. I had the feeling that it was Ma that was holding up my being a partner in the farm. Anyway, Pa and I started planning. We were able to get my uncles, Walt and Ben, to milk the cows for one night. It was the first week in June and our planting was done, so farmwork could wait for a day or two.

The *Racine Daily Journal* ran a full-page article about the fair, and I read every word at least a hundred times. The Union Pacific Railroad had a train called the Zephyr, which had just broken the speed record going from Denver to Chicago in thirteen hours and five minutes. The paper described the train as streamlined; boy, it would be a sight to see. According to the paper, there was to be a new sixteen-cylinder Cadillac on display. Imagine, a sixteen-cylinder car? Lincoln supposedly had a car called the Lincoln-Zephyr that had the engine in the rear. Strange! I couldn't help but notice the blurb about Sally Rand. Sally Rand was a bubble and fan dancer. Apparently, she kept the bubbles and fans in all the right places if you know what I mean. Not that it matters, 'cause Ma would kill me!

Finally, the day came. Pa and Ma hadn't been speaking much, but to Pa's credit, he never changed his mind about going. We got up even earlier than usual and got all the chores done. Pa said to Ma, "Are you coming?" A frosty *no* was the response. Pa and I dressed in our Sunday best, I drove the Buick to the train station in Sturtevant, and we were off on our adventure.

The train pulled into the Union Station about 9:00 a.m., and we walked a few blocks to the fair or, should I say, the Century of Progress, which was the official name. We were both stunned by the size of it; we were told that the fair was over four hundred acres! Pa kind of let me set the pace and direction. First, we saw the train and then the Cadillac and the Lincoln. Then I was fascinated by a gate with the word "Odditorium."

"Come on, Pa, let's go!"

And so we did. Each of the acts costs ten cents. First we saw the Two-Headed Baby, then the Alligator Man, and then Zeno the Australian Snake Eater. The first two looked pretty fake. The baby had a growth on its neck, but I certainly wouldn't call it another head. The alligator man looked like somebody had painted scales on his body. But boy, oh boy, Zeno the Australian Snake Eater put on a show.

Zeno had a barker at the entrance to the tent. The barker had a megaphone, and it sounded like this, "Ladies and gentlemen, you will be amazed, alarmed, and afraid. Zeno eats rattlesnakes for breakfast,

JAMES R. VYVYAN SR.

lunch, and dinner. For just ten cents, you will see a show that will haunt you forever! The show starts in two minutes. Come on in!"

Going in, I was afraid it would be fake like the other two. Boy, was I wrong. We were sitting in the front row. Zeno came out, and he was at least six feet tall with rippling muscles and a bronze tan. He was dressed in some very skimpy shorts, sandals, and headdress like an Indian snake charmer. He first brought out a brownish snake about two feet long and played with it like it was a pet. He wrapped it around his arm, leg, and neck. I thought it was exciting, but part of me was saying, "The barker said *eat* and *rattlesnake*, and I know this is nothing but a common milk snake." Just as that thought went through my head, Zeno ate the head right off that snake! The crowd kind of went "Oooooh." Maybe thirty seconds later, someone behind me yelled, "That's no rattlesnake, that's a simple milk snake." Zeno kind of grinned and slowly pulled the canvas cover off a cage to his left. Sure enough, inside was a rattlesnake, and he was rattling up a storm. Zeno opened the cage and cautiously reached in and grabbed the snake. You could tell he was much more careful about how he handled this snake. He wasn't wrapping it around any part of his body. The crowd went quiet as he slowly brought the snake toward his face, and with a catlike move, he bit the head clean off! No, he didn't eat the snake, but he bit the head of that rattler clean off! I looked at Pa, and we were both speechless.

Pa and I walked out of Zeno's tent totally amazed. Next, Pa said he wanted to see Homes of Tomorrow. I kind of thought this was to have something significant to tell Ma. I didn't object. Many of the houses were something called art deco, which I didn't appreciate. I did appreciate the one house that had a personal helicopter pad! Also, some of the homes were prefabs, something I had never heard of. In the same vein, we visited the agriculture building and the dairy building.

As we left the dairy building, Pa caught sight of a sign advertising the Garland sisters, featuring a ten-year-old Judy Garland. Apparently, Pa had heard of this group, and they were good.

The next thing we saw was the entrance to the Sally Rand Show. I looked at Pa, but I didn't say a word. Pa smiled and said, "You only live once!" I thought my heart was going to stop. Sally Rand, the bubble dancer! I'm going to see Sally Rand, the famous bubble dancer! Some say she was naked, some say she had some parts covered with a flesh-colored material. We weren't close enough to tell. I can tell you it was an exciting show, and the way she tried to keep the bubbles over the important places was a work of art.

I could tell you much more, but I'll just end with "It was fantastic!"

There was one more fantastic thing that happened in 1933. It was two days before Thanksgiving, and Pa and I were just finishing harvesting the corn north of the house, when a 1933 Buick 90 stopped by the side of the road. As a young man, I was pretty excited to see such a beautiful car. It put Pa's old Buick to shame. Anyway, out of the car popped six men in suits, and one of them approached us. "Our car is running pretty hot. I was wondering if I could bother you to get us a little water. Be happy to pay you for your trouble."

Pa replied, "You don't need to pay us. Tom, would you run back to the house and bring out a gallon of water?"

"Sure, Pa." I ran and got the water, and when I got back the hood of the Buick was open, and there was steam coming from the radiator. "Here's the water, mister."

The guy started pouring the water into the radiator, and Pa jumped in. "None of my business, but you're likely to crack the block if you pour that cold water in a hot engine like that." The guy in the suit slowed pouring the water to a trickle.

As I watched, I noticed water dripping from a spot in the lower right corner of the radiator. "Hey, mister, I think you got a hole in your radiator."

There was no reply, and he thanked us and, when Pa wasn't looking, stuffed something into my pocket. In a flash, they were in the car and off they went. It was after Thanksgiving that we got word that the Racine Bank and Trust Company had been robbed by the Dillinger gang in a 1933 Buick 90. Pa and I are darn right sure that was a bullet hole in the radiator, and by the way, it was a ten dollar bill.

CHAPTER ELEVEN

The Glider

AFTER RETURNING FROM Chicago, things got back to normal. Ma and Pa seemed to go back to their usual routine. However, since the mortgage was paid off, I felt a little more freedom to have some fun. I got together with a group of friends—Wes Vivian, Willie Young, and Goldie Shepherd—and formed a kind of club. We started going for Sunday rides on our horses and then a few dances in Union Grove. One day Goldie announced that he had sent to Germany for plans to build a glider. We were dumbstruck. I said, "What do you know about building a glider?"

Wes piped up with, "We're smart. I guess we can do whatever we set our minds to!"

Willie wondered, "What would it cost?" We decided to wait and see what the plans were like.

Two weeks later the plans arrived, but they were in German! We only knew one German family, the Reuls, so we enlisted their help in translating the plans. It took Dick Reul about a week to get them translated to his satisfaction. Then the four club members sat down for a look-see. First, the plans stated that the material would cost about $35. We felt the four of us could come up with that amount. Second, it was big with a wingspan of twenty-eight feet. Where would we build it? Wes thought there was room in the haymow of his barn if we built it in three pieces—two wings and the center section. The materials seemed like they were readily available, just fir strips, linen thread, light canvas, and some cable. So that winter, we spent nearly every Sunday afternoon working on our glider.

Come spring, word got around about our glider. I don't think anyone in Yorkville had ever ridden in a plane, and some people had never even seen a plane. So our glider was quite a sensation and the talk of the neighborhood. We decided the hayfield east of my house would be perfect for our first flight, and we set Sunday, May 7, at 2:00 p.m. for our first voyage. I was to hook our Buick up to the plane and accelerate to thirty miles per hour and then I would signal the pilot, Goldie, to unhook the tow rope.

The seventh turned out to be a perfect day with temperatures around seventy degrees and almost no wind. We started assembling the three pieces of the glider, and by 1:00 p.m., it looked ready. What surprised us was that a crowd of nearly 150 people had gathered and was still growing. People were picnicking in our hayfield, and we felt like real celebrities. We were also pretty nervous, although we tried to look like we were calm and collected. Willie squeaked, "What if this thing doesn't fly?"

Goldie piped in, "What if it does? I'm the pilot, and I'm not sure I can land it. I wish it had wheels instead of skids!"

Thanks to the Oak Clearing Museum

I backed the Buick up to the glider and hooked on to the tow rope. Ever so slowly I moved forward, taking the slack out of the rope. Goldie gave me the thumbs up, and I lurched forward. About five seconds into the run, I started to wish I had someone else in the Buick so I could look where I was going and the other person could watch the glider.

JAMES R. VYVYAN SR.

Five miles per hour and the glider is still sliding along the grass. Ten miles per hour and it started to lift off. When I reached twenty, I could no longer see the glider, and I saw the tow rope fall to the ground, and then a scream and a big crunch.

I looked back and saw that I had run over a picnic basket, but more importantly, the glider was nearly forty feet high! It did a perfect 180 and came down nearly at the starting point, pitching forward and dumping Goldie onto the ground. Everyone ran to the glider and was shouting, "Goldie, are you okay?" I got there first because I drove. I helped Goldie to his feet. I could tell he was hurting, but there was no way he was going to let the crowd know that. "Goldie, I thought the plans said that the pilot could only control the altitude. How the hell did you make that turn?"

"I have no idea!"

Then I let the rest of the crowd congratulate him.

I started to think about the picnic basket. I slowly walked back to the spot of the accident, wondering how I was going to handle this. Standing by the smashed basket was Ann Hansen, a girl I had danced with a few weeks earlier. "You owe me a new basket, Mr. Foxwell."

"I sure do. I'm just glad it wasn't you that I ran over."

That's how it started. Ann and I became what you call an item. The Sunday afternoons working on the glider were replaced with Sunday afternoons with Ann. At our first kiss, I knew I was a goner. She introduced me to all kinds of things. She liked to dance, and I found myself traveling to Milwaukee and Chicago hearing Lawrence Welk, Ozzie Nelson, and Duke Ellington. If you had told me last year that I would travel that far to dance, I would have called you crazy. She also told me that I should call my ma and pa, Mom and Dad, not entirely sure why.

Like I said, I knew I was a goner at our first kiss. In two months, I asked her to marry me, and two months later, we were married. I'm the happiest man alive!

CHAPTER TWELVE

Ann

MY SISTER, GLORIA, and I were raised on a farm about two miles south of Union Grove. I'm nineteen, and Gloria is eighteen. Our dad is a farmer and a blacksmith. He spends the majority of his time fixing machinery and putting new points on plowshares. Our mom works at home, and I think she's a great cook and mother. Gloria and I grew up working on the farm, so we know hard work and we know farming. Our parents encouraged us to go to Union Grove High School, and we both graduated. Since graduation, I've been working as a maid for Gene, a retired bachelor. It's not bad, but there is certainly no future in it.

I've been told that I'm smart and pretty. I know I did all right in high school, and I know I'm not ugly; but I'm not so sure I'm pretty. (I think I have a nice shape, if I do say so myself.) I'm a little shy, but I know what I want and I'm willing to work for it. I've always wanted to be a mother and a farm wife. That's what I know, and that's what I like.

This brings us to the dance this April in Union Grove. I wore my new blue dress with lace trim around the neck and sleeves and a pleated skirt. Gloria and I were there early, and I noticed Tom Foxwell the moment he walked in the door. He was far and away the most handsome man at the dance. A couple of girls asked him to dance, but I noticed that he only asked me and one other girl to dance. I could tell he was shy, but he was able to say, "That's a beautiful dress you're wearing."

So on May 7, yes, I was interested in the glider, but I had more interest in Tom. I didn't mean for my picnic basket to be run over, but I did put myself and the basket in a place that we'd be noticed. I was not unhappy when the basket got run over because I knew that Tom and I would have a talk.

It turned out to be much more than a talk, and Tom turned out to be more than just handsome. Tom is honest, hardworking, caring, and a good man. He's a little shy, but so am I. Tom is a man of few words, but when he says something, he means it. I'm head over heels in love with this man. He's what I've always dreamed of.

I know he loves me completely and for all the right reasons. But here's the thing. I've been dreaming of being married and having children all my life. It seems like Tom has never thought of being married until he met me. We had a wonderful time dating. He took me to so many great places. We had great fun. When he asked me to marry him, there was only one possible answer. A few days later, I asked him, "Where will we live?"

"Well, ah, I haven't thought about that."

"I don't have any money, do you?"

"I could ask Dad for a raise."

And so it went. Tom has been so busy with the farm, he's only recently thought about married life.

Eventually, Tom came to me with an idea. "Mom, Dad, and I have talked it over, and we could live where the maid has been living. Mom is going to do without a maid, and we could live in the portion of the house that she lived in."

My brain did a little flip-flop. Let me see, his mom is going to do without a maid; does that mean I'll be the maid? I've heard and witnessed some things concerning his mom that scare me. But what do I say? I'm not a complainer; again there was only one answer, "Great!"

Before we were married, I got up the courage to say to Tom, "How long do you think you'll remain a hired man on the farm?" I knew that someday he would inherit the farm, being the only child. But the small amount he was being paid by his parents would make our life pretty difficult.

His response was "Gee, I really don't know. I've asked that question a couple of times and haven't gotten much of an answer."

Tom's aunts gave us a beautiful wedding shower, and before I knew it, it was our wedding day. We got married in the Paris Methodist Church, and my sister was my bridesmaid. Tom asked Mack Moyle to be his best man. We didn't have a honeymoon; there was hay to put up.

One thing I haven't told Tom—in fact, I haven't told anyone—I think I'm pregnant. I'm wondering how Tom will react. I predict he'll be speechless but happy. He probably hasn't thought much about being a dad either. I'm already thinking about naming the baby either John, after my dad, or Esther, from the Bible.

CHAPTER THIRTEEN

The Pregnancy

IT SEEMS I got pregnant almost immediately. I don't think we'd been married a month before I realized that I was pregnant. This certainly wasn't part of the plan. If I had my druthers, we'd have waited and gotten to know each other a little better, but that was not to be.

You can't imagine what it's like to be pregnant and have twelve consecutive days over one hundred degrees! The perspiration just rolls off me. I'd like to just soak in a tub of cold water, but carrying that cold water to the tub is more than I can do. But I'm no weakling; I can take the heat. That's really not what's bothering me.

After we got married, my parents would often invite us over for Sunday dinner. After a couple of times, we reciprocated and had them over to our house for dinner. Tom's family is so different. We live on opposite sides of the same house. Wouldn't you think that occasionally we would have a meal together? After eight months, I thought I would try to change things. So I invited Grace over for a little lemonade one hot summer day. We sat down at our kitchen table, and before five minutes passed, she said, "Your floor is dirty. You know it'll have to be cleaner than that for the baby." I was nearly eight months pregnant, and scrubbing the floor on my hands and knees in hundred-degree heat was more than I could do. I wanted to just cry, but I held it together and replied, "You're right, and if it cools off tomorrow, I'll get right to it." But Grace wouldn't leave it alone. "You know we share a washing machine, and I expect that you leave it like you find it." I'm a mild-mannered woman, and I can't remember when I've lost my temper, but we finished our lemonade in silence.

I've tried to make allowances for Grace. I know she lost her son, Tom's brother, in that terrible silo accident. They say there is nothing worse than losing a child. However, there seems to be something more going on. Tom has told me that even before Joe died, his mom was cold and strict. He told me about having to dig tile at the age of eight or nine. That doesn't even seem possible.

The added factor in all this is that Grace and Tom Sr. continue to own the entire farm, and Tom Jr. makes $145 a month as their hired man. Tom has talked to them about becoming a partner. Really, he's their only child, and he's going to get the farm sooner or later. It seems cruel to me. I know Tom tempers his comments to them because he wants to be a partner and doesn't want to cause any waves. Where does that leave me? I know he'd like to stand up for me but is held back by this partnership deal and maybe something else. I'm not sure what it is.

Tom Sr. is so different. He has always been nothing but kind to me. Unlike Grace, he stops by our side almost every day after breakfast. He always has something kind to say. Not only do I like him, but I also sense that nearly everyone in Yorkville likes him. I don't understand how he and Grace get along or how they ever got together.

I love my husband, yet he's a mix of his parents. Physically he takes the best of both parents. He certainly is better looking than either of his parents. Emotionally, he tends to be more like his dad. He's unfailingly kind and loving to me. Yet he does have difficulty expressing his feelings and his love. He's a man of few words. I predicted he'd be happy when I told him of my pregnancy but wouldn't know what to say. I was mostly right. "Honey, I'm going to have a baby."

A big smile spread across his face, and he said, "I'm gonna go buy him a horse!"

I sure didn't predict that response, and I don't know why he assumed it was going to be a boy.

Enough about the Foxwell family. Tom and I have decided to have the baby at St. Mary's Hospital in Racine. Our baby will be the first one in the family to be born in a hospital. It seems to be all the rage. Fewer and fewer babies are born at home. I guess at least partially because fewer and fewer doctors will make house calls. I'm excited and scared. I've heard so many stories about difficult births. I've tried to put these stories out of my mind, but they keep creeping back in.

CHAPTER FOURTEEN

The Birth

PEOPLE HAVE BEEN teasing me because I bought a horse for our son before he was born. They're also teasing me because I keep referring to our child as a "he." I'm not sure why I've been doing that, it just seems so natural.

Last Tuesday, Ann poked me at 2:11 a.m., and she said, "It's time." Driving to St. Mary's Hospital, it's difficult to describe how I felt. I'm sure my heart was beating a mile a minute, but I wasn't panicking. I drove the speed limit, and there was literally no traffic.

Dr. Niess was waiting for us, and we checked into a room with two beds. The second bed was occupied by Karen Beaumont another Yorkville person. Dr. Niess examined Ann and said we'd just have to wait. Her contractions were about twenty minutes apart. They put a heart monitor on Ann's stomach to monitor the baby. After about two hours, the monitor started beeping, and no heartbeat was shown on the monitor. *Oh my god*, I thought, *I could take the loss, but what will I tell Ann?*

A nurse came in, made a minor adjustment, and the beeping stopped, and the heart rhythm reappeared. However, my heartbeat and blood pressure, I'm sure, were off the charts. Twenty-four hours later, not much had changed. Dr. Niess came in and examined Ann again. This time he looked worried. "The baby's heartbeat has slowed considerably. We need to take action."

As they wheeled Ann out of the room, I was worried but was very glad that we were at a hospital and not at home. I had regained a certain calmness. I knew that it was out of my hands. I really only panic when I'm the one that's on the hot seat, when I'm the one that has an impact on the outcome. I would be lousy working in an emergency room.

It was hours before I heard any news. Eventually, Dr. Niess appeared looking exhausted. "Tell me, Doc!"

"You have a beautiful eight-pound one-ounce baby boy."

"Thank God!"

"Your wife, on the other hand, has been through a lot. She'll need to remain in the hospital for some time. I hesitate to tell you this, but it's likely she won't have any more children."

"Can I see my wife?"

"Yes, certainly, but don't stay very long."

As I approached my wife, she whispered, "Is the baby okay?"

"Yes, dear, we have a beautiful baby boy." I said that even though I hadn't seen the baby yet.

"Can we name him John, after my dad?"

"Of course." I thought to myself, *We already have me, Tom Jr. We certainly don't need another Tom.*

"Have you called the grandparents?"

"Not yet."

"Tell them I'm not up to company."

So I was right all along, our baby is a boy. It's been a week, and Ann is still in the hospital. The doctor made it clear that she was not to be left alone for at least a month. I thought for a second—well, my mom will be right next door; she won't be alone. Then I realized how stupid that sounded, given the relationship between Mom and Ann. I quickly called Ann's mom, and she readily agreed to stay with us for the month.

I wonder what kind of dad I'll be. I know, and Ann knows, that I'll do my best, but will my best be good enough?

CHAPTER FIFTEEN

What a Year

FEBRUARY 7, 1936, was the first indication of what kind of year this was going to be. It started snowing about 2:00 p.m., lightly at first, and then the wind and snow picked up at a mighty pace. In the next twenty-four hours, we had over twenty-eight inches of snow with gale force winds of more than forty miles per hour. Blizzard! I know blizzards are awful things and people die because of them, but there is something terribly exciting about them. Maybe it's the challenge of man versus nature or knowing that one mistake could cost you your life. All I know is that it invigorates me and, at the same time, scares the hell out of me.

The wind stayed strong for two days, whipping the snow into drifts eight or nine feet tall. I'm not sure you know what this means for a dairy farm. Our first thoughts were to protect the animals from freezing. Normally sheep, pigs, and cows can spend winter outside if they have food, water, and a windbreak. This was an exception. The heavy snow, strong winds, and falling temperatures could cause death. We had to crowd the animals into our barn and outbuildings. This was no small task. Neither man nor beast could see the door or each other. Once I looked at Dad and his eyebrows and eyelashes had a dozen icicles hanging from them; I don't know how he could see a thing. I must have looked the same. When we came in for supper, our clothes were frozen stiff, and we hung them by the stove to thaw out. Dad didn't say much, with one significant exception, "Tom, just remember: men make plans and God laughs."

Feeding and watering the animals was an enormous task. Try carrying two five-gallon pails of water through snow up to your waist. After dumping the water into the trough, it would freeze solid in less than an hour, so if the animals didn't drink quickly, they were out of luck. Plus, it's not beyond imagination that one of us could get lost just trudging the fifty yards from the barn to one of the outbuildings. As the wind settled down, we shoveled paths from the house to the barn and the outbuildings.

As we milked the cows, the barn creaked and groaned from the wind. It sounded like rusty nails being pulled from dry wood. As we finished milking, another problem presented itself. We have enough milk cans to keep the milk for two days. The roads have now been closed for two days, and it's likely they will be closed for three or four more days. Normally, we load the cans on a wagon and take them to the creamery. This is not possible now. We can't afford to dump the milk; money is too tight. Our next option is to hook my horse, Pepper, up to the sleigh and take the milk to the creamery. At first, you'd think this would be an easy solution. It is not. Neither Pepper nor any other horse can pull a sleigh through these huge drifts.

**Image property of Racine Heritage Museum
archival collection (all rights reserved)**

With no other option, Pepper and I started out toward the creamery, planning to weave a course around the drifts. The drifting had stopped, but I spent a good deal of time off the road trying to find a path with the least amount of snow. A couple of times, I misjudged the depth of the snow, and Pepper found himself up to his belly and unable to move.

Then I had to get off the sleigh, dig Pepper out, and lead him on to a more manageable path. One time, as I was digging Pepper out, I caught my mitten on one of the harness buckles and ripped it open. The good news is that I made it home, but when my hand thawed out, blisters as much as an inch across popped up on the exposed skin. As it turns out, when the snow plows did come, the snow was so deep they couldn't make it through. The whole community got together and shoveled. What else will this year bring?

I probably should mention our wedding. Ann would probably tell you about the beautiful music and dresses. I, however, have a little different memory. Our wedding was scheduled for 2:00 p.m. At 10:00 a.m., it was clear that one of our best heifers was trying to have calf. Heifers often have a difficult time giving birth, but this one was worse. The calf was coming backward. We tried our usual method. We tied baling twine on to two legs and attached the other end of the twine to a heavy wooden handle. Dad and I pulled on that handle for all we were worth. No luck.

We then called our vet, Doc Bukel. He arrived about 11:30 a.m. He attached light chains to the legs and attached the other end of the chains to a device similar to a bumper jack. This device rested on the heifer's hips. As he was working, he liked to talk. He told us one of his clients died on Monday. To the family's displeasure, a neighboring farmer showed up on Tuesday trying to rent the farm. Apparently, the fight for good farmland was getting fierce. I couldn't believe farmers could be so insensitive. At first I welcomed something to do to keep me from getting too nervous, but by 12:30 p.m., I was really nervous, and finally Doc said, "We can handle this, you'd better go."

That's when things turned for the worse. I showered, shaved, and started to get ready. Earlier in the day, my best man had taken my travel bag to the hotel. Somehow my wedding shoes and socks were in that bag. Shit! I jumped in the car and drove eighty miles per hour to Hank's Tog Shop in Union Grove. I got some socks, and they luckily had a pair of dress shoes that fit. By the time I got to the church, it was 1:50 p.m. My best man thought I had changed my mind about the wedding. Luckily, he kept the news of my absence from Ann. Oh yes, the heifer survived; the calf did not.

The economy is still in terrible shape. A couple of years ago, Franklin Roosevelt helped get the Agricultural Adjustment Act (AAA) passed. This act paid farmers not to plant corn and wheat and to cut back on the production of milk. This not only put money directly into the farmer's hands; it also reduced the surplus of these items, which helped increase the price farmers received at market. Also, prices were supported by the federal government. If the price of wheat, corn, or milk fell below a certain level, the government would make up the difference. This led to more money in the farmer's pocket and, hopefully, more money for the hired man (me).

But in the meantime, some farmers joined the National Farm Holiday Association. Their plan was to dump their milk, leading to a shortage and, therefore, higher prices. Dad and I went to several such meetings at Yorkville School, but

Dad and I decided we work too hard and are just too tight to dump our milk—no matter how low the price. This led to some hard feelings between us and some of our neighbors who were dumping their milk. There were some tense times, and we would often get the "stink eye" from some friends—especially the Gorzky family. (Dad has told me something about an ice harvesting accident and the resulting hard feelings involving the Gorzkys.) As bad as it is in Yorkville, Racine appears to be far worse. I heard the commentator on the radio referring to Racine as Little Moscow because of all the strikes and labor unrest going on. I'm sure glad we live out here.

Another government program affecting our community is the Works Progress Administration (WPA). This program hires men and women to do projects that benefit the community. The men and women are paid by the federal government. This takes many people off the long list of the unemployed. I've heard some people refer to the WPA as "we piddle around"; boy, that sure isn't true in Yorkville. The WPA workers in Yorkville are digging a basement under Yorkville School by *hand*! My uncle Walt, the family mathematician, claims they are removing over three hundred tons of dirt to complete the basement. It's hard to imagine these people digging and hauling all that dirt one wheelbarrow at a time. I know some people are embarrassed to be employed by the WPA, but they sure are doing a service for Yorkville and Yorkville School. Already, two generations of Foxwells have graduated from Yorkville School. Who knows how many more generations will graduate from there. In addition, Yorkville School used to be heated by a wood-burning stove. The WPA is adding an automatic furnace, fueled by coal in the new basement.

This furnace requires electricity, and President Roosevelt recently signed the Rural Electrification Agency (REA) bill. It's difficult to explain what the REA means to farm people, especially to people who have always lived in the city and have always had electricity. The REA provides grants and low-interest loans to bring electricity to rural America.

This means so much to us and our neighbors. Up until now, we have used a combination of candles, lanterns, and battery power to light our home. When our house was built, it was wired for battery-powered lights. Each of the battery-powered lights provides approximately the light of two lanterns. We have a generator powered by a hit-and-miss engine in our basement to recharge the batteries. Replacing all three of these forms of light with electric light makes a huge difference. I think that each of us has better spirits, more energy, and is happier with the increased light. This is especially true on long winter nights. The electrification of our house didn't happen without some trepidation. My mom, Grace, complained loudly that we were going to burn the house down. I remember her saying, "The wires in these walls were designed for battery power, not this newfangled electricity. Those wires are going to heat up and burn the house down with all that new power." To be honest, I had some of the same fears but kept them to myself.

Another huge difference brought by the REA is water on demand. Up until the tornado, our water was pumped by our windmill. When that was blown down, we replaced it with a hit-and-miss engine and pump. To get water, we would have to go down into the well pit, start the engine, and carry the water to the house. For the cows, we had a tank in the haymow that would be filled by the hit-and-miss engine and gravity fed to the cows. With the coming of electricity, all we have to do is turn the tap in the kitchen. What a difference! The other great advantage is that with water on demand, we can have a toilet in the house and get rid of the outhouse!

Earlier I mentioned the new furnace in Yorkville School. This could not have happened without the REA. Let me explain. Up until now, our home was heated by three woodstoves. Mom and Dad's kitchen and Ann and my kitchen have wood-burning stoves for heat. There is also a wood-burning stove in the basement. These three stoves take an enormous amount of wood. We have a woodshed about fourteen by sixteen feet, and we fill this to a height of ten feet, and even that is not enough wood. Dad and I spend at least a week each year on opposite ends of a two-man crosscut saw cutting logs into lengths small enough to fit in the stoves. I still feel the rhythm of the crosscut saw and Dad saying repeatedly, "Pull, don't push!" Plus, at least another week is spent splitting these logs. Even with all this work, the only truly warm rooms in the house are the two kitchens. In extremely cold weather, we've been known to sleep in the kitchens and close off the unused rooms. Our bedrooms often get *below* freezing. This is because without electricity, there is no fan to blow what little heat there is into the bedrooms. As an example, in the winter, we keep a chamber pot in our bedrooms because it is simply too cold to go to the outhouse. Some mornings, the chamber pots are frozen!

Electricity will allow us to put in a stoker furnace. This furnace will automatically feed coal into the burner, and the fan and duct work will force the heat into all the rooms of the house. No more freezing bedrooms! No more weeks of cutting and splitting wood. What a difference! Of course, this, along with all the other improvements, will cost money, and we can't do everything at once.

Another huge advantage of having electricity is we can get rid of the icebox and replace it with a refrigerator. Gone will be the days of cutting ice out of the neighborhood ponds. Plus, our food will stay colder and, therefore, won't spoil like it used to. Along with the refrigerator, we can get an electric washing machine. No more scrubbing and kneading the clothes and wringing them out by hand.

With electricity, we can now have a real radio. Up until now, I have had a crystal set radio. A crystal set needs neither battery nor AC electricity. It is powered by the radio waves themselves. It didn't produce very much volume and I had to use a headset to hear, but it did pick up a few radio stations in the area. It sure was better than nothing. Now we have a real radio powered by electricity. Since headphones aren't necessary, the whole family can sit around and listen. Our favorite programs are *The Jack Benny Show* and *Here's Gracie* with Jack Benny. The radio sure makes a difference on a cold or stormy night.

At the same time that we brought electricity into the house, we also had a telephone installed. However, I understand our phone is a little different from the phones they have in the cities. To save money, our phone is a party line, and we have it installed between Mom and Dad's side of the house and our side of the house so both families can have access. The party line feature means that there are six families sharing the same phone line. It works like this: Our ring is one long and one short. Our next-door neighbor's, the Vanswols, ring is two longs. The idea is that each of the six parties sharing the line has a different ring. So when the phone rings, you have to listen carefully to tell whether the call is for you or one of the neighbors. This has an unintended consequence that embarrasses me to no end. My mom spends a good deal of her time listening to the conversations of the other people on the party line. This is how it works. The phone rings with two longs. So we know this call is for the Vanswols, not us, but Mom will quietly pick up the receiver and listen to their conversation! I think some of our neighbors have caught on to her because if Dad would yell "Grace, I need you!" it would be obvious to the Vanswols or any of the other four parties that Grace was listening.

The REA and electricity make a tremendous difference to the farm too! It won't happen for a while because of the expense, but with water on demand, all our animals can be watered automatically. Some of the farm magazines even mention something called a barn cleaner. Apparently, the electricity powers a chain-and-paddle device that automatically takes the manure out of the gutters and into the manure spreader. But most importantly is that now we can have milking machines! Up until now, two men could milk about fifteen cows, but two men with milking machines can milk thirty or forty cows in less time. Electricity is a wonderful thing!

The year 1936 brought more weather problems. We planted our crops in a timely fashion in soil with adequate moisture from all the snow, but then it turned hot and dry. We had twelve days in a row with the temperature over a hundred degrees with no rain and no relief. The corn leaves shriveled, the oats turned brown, and the hay never got over six inches tall. Seemed like there was a constant wind from the southwest, and many days the sky was brown. If we left one of the cars outside, it would be covered in dust by morning. Since the windows in the house are open, everything inside is covered with dirt. People are talking about something called the dust bowl and that the dirt is coming from as far as five hundred miles away.

I have to admit that farmers like to complain. It's too hot, too cold, too wet, or too dry. But this time there really is something to complain about and the moods of our two families suffered because of it. After a dozen days with temperatures above a hundred degrees and nightly temperatures never falling below eighty, tempers were starting to fray. Add to that the sight of the crops that you've worked so hard on and depend on to survive shriveling up. The most obvious display of temper was between Ann and my mom. My mom let Ann know that she wasn't keeping our side of the house clean enough and she wasn't keeping the washing machine that they shared clean. Oh boy! Ann came to me crying. How do I handle this? Mom doesn't take criticism well, yet I love my wife with all my heart. Plus, Mom and Dad control the purse strings. I've been waiting for the day when they will make me a partner in the farm rather than a hired man. This sure does complicate things.

I'd like to be able to tell you that I marched into Mom's side of the house and said, "My wife is number one. It's none of your business how she keeps our house. You treat her with respect or we're done!" Like I said, I'd like to tell you that. The thought of losing the farm and delaying my chance to be a partner in it was too strong. Instead, I said to Ann, "That's just the way she is," and to my mom I said nothing. Relaying this story embarrasses me, and I feel like less of the man that I thought I was.

Good news! Just when we thought all was lost, our corner of the state got a million-dollar rain. It started on a Friday with a steady rain. It grew overnight into a heavy rain and continued for two days. We got a total of four inches of rain. Not only would there be something to harvest, but because most of the rest of the nation was in severe drought, the prices were improving. Not only would we survive, but we could start purchasing some of the things that electricity now allowed.

So we all survived 1936. Are we better off for the struggle? I'm not so sure. The constant struggle of surviving on a hired man's wage and trying to keep my wife happy and hasten the time when I'll be a partner in the farm is wearing on me. Is the struggle for the farm worth it? Will Ann and I be better off elsewhere? But where? I didn't go to high school; I don't know anything but farming. Where will this end?

JAMES R. VYVYAN SR.

CHAPTER SIXTEEN

A Mystery Times Two

IT WAS SUNDAY, October 30, 1938. There was a warm southerly wind blowing, and the leaves were falling at a rapid pace. I had all I could do to keep myself from jumping in the sweet-smelling leaves under our giant maple trees. It had been a good fall. The harvest was good, and the grain prices were improved. Dad and I had finished the harvest in record time, and it was time for a little relaxation. Mom had invited the family to a harvest dinner. In attendance were, of course, my wife, Ann, and our newly ambulatory child, John. Aunt Mame and Rocky were there, as were uncles Ben and Walter. Uncle Ben had one married son, Robert, and a grandson, Mark. Uncle Walt had two married sons and two grandchildren, Ben and Atticus. All in all, there must have been about twenty people.

Mom roasted two of our prize geese, and accompanying the dinner were her special English bread pudding, corn casserole, mashed potatoes, and her best apple pie with homemade ice cream for dessert. Everybody was in a good mood as the pressures of harvest were at an end. Dinner talk centered on a little good-natured bragging about who had the best yielding corn. Then the talk turned to the labor troubles at Nash in Racine and Kenosha. In fact, we had just learned that Nash in Racine had closed. Rocky was sure the unions were the cause of all the problems. Uncle Ben wasn't so sure; in fact, he thought that the Nash cars just weren't very good.

To lighten the mood, Uncle Ben told the joke about the farmer and the airplane. "A farmer and his wife went to the fair and were fascinated by the airplane rides. The farmer asked the pilot how much for a ride. The pilot responded, 'Ten dollars for the both of you.' The farmer said, 'That's too much.' The pilot said, 'I'll make you a deal, if you can make it through the whole ride without saying a word, the ride is free, otherwise you'll have to pay me ten bucks.' After the ride, the pilot congratulated the farmer for not saying a word. The farmer replied, 'Thanks, but I gotta tell you I almost screamed when my wife fell out.'"

Not to be outdone, Uncle Walt started in. "Did you hear about Mr. and Mrs. Deering out in Burlington? Mrs. Deering was arrested for stealing a can of peaches and had to appear before the judge. The judge said, 'I'm sentencing you to six days in jail, one for each peach in the can.' Mr. Deering slowly raised his hand, 'Judge, she also stole a can of peas.'"

Of course, now it was my dad's turn. "Did you hear that Doc Moyle was injured this week? He was helping dig a new well, and it caved in on him. He should have cared for the sick and left the well alone!"

I could see that Aunt Mame's husband, Rocky, was squirming uncomfortably. Every other male of his generation had told a joke, and I could tell he could feel the pressure. Finally he started. "Mame and I have had a few good years." I could tell everybody was uncomfortable. What was he saying? He and Mame have had a few good years? If I know Mame, she's going to box his ears when they get home. He continued, "Yeah, we have a couple Goodyear tires on the truck, four on our tractor, and a couple on the old Ford." Everybody breathed a sigh of relief and had a good laugh.

It was about 7:00 p.m., and the sun was setting. Dad suggested we roast a few marshmallows. We all gathered around a fire just south of the woodshed. It was quite a sight. The full moon was rising, warm south wind blowing, and lots of happy talk. Around five to eight, someone, I don't recall who, said, "Let's listen to the *Edgar Bergen and Charlie McCarthy Show.*" My wife, Ann, said, "Or we could listen to my cousin, Orson, from Kenosha, on WTMJ."

The Edgar Bergen fans won out, and at 8:00 p.m., the adults gathered round the radio to hear Edgar Bergen and Charlie McCarthy. Charlie McCarthy, if you don't know, was a wooden dummy, and Edgar Bergen was a ventriloquist. We were enjoying the show until Mae West came on and Charlie said to her, "Don't tell that story. All my girlfriends are listening." Mae West replied, "You're all wood and a yard long." Some of the family were offended, and Dad piped up, "Let's turn on WTMJ and listen to Ann's cousin Orson from Kenosha." Nobody complained.

But it wasn't Orson's voice we heard. A band was playing "Stardust," which we all enjoyed. Then the music was interrupted, "Huge explosions have been seen on the planet Mars. Nothing like this has ever been seen before!" The music continued. Then a second interruption, "A huge flaming object has fallen on a farm in Trenton, New Jersey." The music continued. A third interruption, "A gigantic metal cylinder has been discovered in Grover's Mill, New Jersey. It is more than thirty yards across. Scientists say that the metal casing is most certainly extraterrestrial." We were beyond interested, and it seemed very odd that there had been no commercials or station identifications. Then the music stopped for good, and it was all news.

"A heat ray has burned hundreds of individuals beyond recognition."

"A unit of 7,000 national guard soldiers has been destroyed with only 120 survivors."

"More cylinders have been discovered in other states!"

Now we were becoming worried. Could this be real? If it wasn't real, surely there would be commercials and station identifications. But there were none. Dad called the rest of the family in from the bonfire. I noticed his shotgun was at the ready. Could this be real? It had been thirty minutes with no commercials or station IDs, what was going on? Finally, at 8:40 p.m., Ann's cousin, Orson Welles, came on and said, "This is the *Mercury Theater on the Air* bringing you, *The War of the Worlds* by H. G. Wells."

That put us at ease, and we all took a deep breath. We returned to the bonfire just as our blood pressures started to recede. Then we saw something that we couldn't believe. While we were all inside, leaves had caught on fire and the south wind pushed the fire right up to the south wall of the woodshed, blackening the wooden siding. There was a five-gallon pail right next to the fire. It hadn't been there earlier. It was obvious that someone had been dipping water out of the stock tank and throwing it on the fire. But who? We were all inside listening to Orson Welles.

The answer to that question would haunt us for a long time. We didn't tell people outside of the family for fear they wouldn't believe us or, worse yet, think we were crazy. Still the question remained.

We did talk to the neighbors that had been listening to the radio Sunday night. Most of them started listening to *Mercury Theater on the Air* from the beginning and knew it was just a story. But there were a few, like us, that tuned in late and, if they were honest, were frightened or at least momentarily confused.

For the next year, every time we gathered, someone would bring up the fire. Most of us believe it was one of Uncle Walter's or Uncle Ben's grandchildren that snuck out of the house during the excitement, started the fire by accident, and then worked to put it out. But if that's the case none of them were brave enough to admit it.

CHAPTER SEVENTEEN

World War II

OUR SON, JOHN, was just three when war broke out in Europe. I was still the hired man for my parents at the paltry sum of $165 a month. The economy was still a mess, and the mood of the country was to avoid war at all costs. I, of course, was at prime draft age, and that worried Ann and me a lot. Some of my friends, like Mack Moyle and Richard Hay, have already volunteered. They told me that another war was a sure thing, and they wanted to be officers by the time it arrived. I, on the other hand, was considering applying for a farm deferment. The farm deferment allows for certain individuals to stay home and grow the food needed for the war effort.

Our mood of avoiding war at all costs changed dramatically one Sunday afternoon as we were listening to the radio. John Daly of CBS interrupted the program, and I remember his words well, "We interrupt this program to bring you a news bulletin. The Japanese have attacked Pearl Harbor, Hawaii, by air, President Roosevelt has just announced." Instantly, this changed everything. Those who have been advocating for staying out of the war were singing a different tune. Suddenly there seemed to be hatred of the Japanese and, to some extent, the Germans. It seemed like nearly everyone was in complete support of going to war against the Japanese and the Germans.

By this time, we had traded the Fordson tractor, and we now had an Allis Chalmers WC and a John Deere A tractor, both of them with rubber tires. We also had a combine and a baler that we pulled behind the WC. It became obvious that the glut of corn, wheat, and milk was over. Since most of Europe was involved in a war, there was suddenly a tremendous shortage of all three commodities. What this meant was that prices were rising and rising significantly.

I felt that Dad and I needed to take advantage of the situation. Dad wasn't so sure. Dad has never had much of a desire for anything since my brother Joe died. I wasn't to be stopped. I rented, on my own, the Gosmire farm and the Schwartz farm. Farming and hard work is all I know, so I saw this as my chance to break away from being a hired man.

As you can imagine, operating these two new farms on my own was not easy. But by the early forties, prices were skyrocketing. I know that my wife and son suffered because I was gone so much, but I was doing this for them. Complicating the matter was that the government instituted rationing. Sugar, gas, butter, meat, tires, silk, shoes, nylon, cars, farm equipment, etc. were all rationed. We were limited to a small amount of each. There were red ration cards for meat, butter, cheese, etc. and blue cards for fruits, vegetables, juices, etc. A lot of this didn't matter to farmers like me because we raised our own meat, butter, cheese, fruits, vegetables, etc. However, there were a few exceptions, notably sugar, tires, and farm equipment.

Sugar was a big problem. All of us enjoy a little sugar. But as they say, where there is a will, there is a way. We started raising sorghum. Sorghum is a tall grasslike plant that grows anywhere from five to eight feet tall. Once the sorghum was mature, we ran it through a machine that cut it into one-inch lengths. We then took it to our neighbor, Walt Vivian, who had an apple cider press. We put the one-inch lengths into the press and out came a sweet liquid. We boiled that liquid down to make it more concentrated; it looked kind of like molasses. We used that concentrated liquid as a substitute for sugar. Did it taste the same as sugar? Not quite, it had a slightly sour taste, but it sure was better than nothing.

Tires were another problem. You basically couldn't get new tires. New tires were all used in the war effort. This came at an unfortunate time, because we had just about converted all our equipment from steel wheels to rubber tires. We probably had thirty or forty rubber tires between our cars and equipment. So what did we do when one went flat? It depends. If it was just a nail in the tire, we removed the tire from the wheel and took the tube up to Felix Peter's service station. Now here was the one pleasant thing about all this. Felix would put what was called a hot patch on the tube. What this meant was he would find the hole in the tube often by inflating the tube and putting it underwater to see where the bubbles emerge. Once the hole was located, he roughened up the rubber with a rasp and placed the hot patch on the offending area. He struck a match, and the hot patch began to burn and weld itself

JAMES R. VYVYAN SR.

to the rubber. You might ask what was the pleasant thing in all this? The scent from the burning adhesives in the hot patch was heavenly, but you didn't want to think too much about how healthy that smoke was for your body.

If the blowout was more serious and the tire itself was damaged, we'd put a boot in the tire. Boots come in various sizes, but the average one is about four-by-five inches. The boot was less than a quarter-inch thick. We put the boot inside the tire to reinforce the area of the tire that was damaged.

The third major problem was the unavailability of farm equipment and cars. This just meant you took tremendous care of your equipment. Equipment that in the past you might have put on the scrap heap now would be repaired endlessly.

Since we had extra ration cards for meat, milk, vegetables, etc., we could use these to bargain for most of the other things that we needed.

I received my farm deferment. I was no longer subject to the draft. This, in itself, caused problems. Some of the neighbors had gotten farm deferments when their farms were really too small to be eligible, or there was plenty of family labor available without giving them a deferment. Many people saw this as unfair. This was not the case for me being the only son on a large dairy farm.

Another problem caused by the farm deferments were the few neighbors whose sons had been drafted and were fighting and dying for our country, while people like me were home safe and sound. I understood that feeling, and I had a little guilt in that regard. However, when I looked at Ann and John and the fact that nearly every morsel of food that we produced was needed for the war effort, that feeling went away quickly.

With all the young men who had gone off to war, there was a real shortage of farm labor. Ann had taken a job at Twin Disc in Racine; she felt the need to do what she could to help the war effort. To my dad's credit, he was good about helping me with the two new farms that I had rented. Still, there was a tremendous amount of work to be done and just the two of us to do it. I longed for the time when our son, John, was old enough to help. Until then, a new solution had appeared. In Sturtevant, there was an encampment of German prisoners of war. The word was you could hire these prisoners for fifty cents an hour, payable to the US government. Of that money, the prisoners received eighty cents a day in coupons that could be used to buy toothpaste, shaving cream, etc.

We had a family meeting to discuss the situation. Dad and I, mostly me at that time, had two hundred acres of corn that needed to be cultivated. If the corn wasn't cultivated soon, the weeds would take over. (We had a cultivator on the WC. Just so you understand, our cultivator did two rows of corn at a time. It consisted of twelve teeth that dig out the weeds between the rows.) Dad and I had sixty acres of hay to put up; no way could we do both. We had an extra bedroom upstairs that wasn't being used. Of course, the safety of our families came first. It was decided that Dad and I would go over to the camp on the next rainy day and take a look-see.

We arrived about 10:00 a.m., and sure enough, there were about 250 tents and about 500 denim-clad men. All the tents were surrounded by mud. We spoke to the lieutenant in charge and explained our situation. The lieutenant said he had just the man for us, and he introduced us to Lukas. He told us that from his experience, he would trust Lukas with his money or his life. "Does this man speak English?"

"A little."

"Does he know how to drive a tractor and cultivate corn?"

The lieutenant spoke, "Wissen Sie, wie um einen Traktor zu fahren?"

"Ja."

I looked at Dad, and he nodded, and so I had my first hired man!

Lukas was about five feet six inches with a slim build and dark hair. My first thought was that he was nothing like the Aryan ideal we've been hearing so much about. His eyes were gray, but his smile was actually quite charming. We wanted to know a little more about Lukas, so we invited our only German neighbor, Dick Reul, to come over and translate. It turned out Lukas lived on the family farm just outside Salzburg, Austria. He had no desire to join the German army, but it was either join or be shot. He told us their farm was about thirty hectares and very hilly. He and his dad grew mostly hay, which they fed to their Holstein cows.

We asked him about his experiences in the war. This was where he became quiet. It was obvious that he didn't want to talk about the war. He simply said as translated, "I fought under Rommel and was captured in the second battle of El Alamein."

Lukas ate his meals with us, and he worked like a slave. He made it clear how grateful he was to be out of the camp and eating good food. He stayed with us for two weeks and cultivated all two hundred acres of corn. He did a tremendous job. If, occasionally, he would get off the corn row, he would stop the tractor and go back and uncover the buried corn by hand. If he accidentally dug a stalk of corn completely out of the ground, he would do his best to transplant it back into the row. He was a real gift from God when we needed one.

Lukas only had one complaint. It became clear that he hated the Allis Chalmers WC. He kept saying, "Hurensohn! Glaubst du, ich habe drei Hande?" We had no idea what he was talking about. Finally Dick Reul translated for us, "Son of a bitch! Do you think I have three hands?" Suddenly it all made sense. The WC is a strange contraption because it has hand brakes instead of foot brakes. It is a little scary because you need to let go of the steering wheel to apply the brakes.

Lukas taught us a thing or two. If nothing else, it made us realize that the soldiers on the other side were not that much different from us. They had families, who they love and just wanted to tend their farms like Dad and I wanted to. The next time I saw one of the crazy, demeaning caricatures of a Japanese soldier or a German soldier, I thought of Lukas and a feeling of sadness came over me.

There was one slightly amusing thing that happened in WWII. On March 14, the county agent organized a meeting of all the local farmers at Yorkville School. We all sat down, and the county agent explained that the government had asked him to show us a movie. So we all sat back, and the title of the movie was *Hemp for Victory*. Apparently, the government wanted all of us to grow hemp. Heck, I didn't even know what hemp was until I watched the movie. It turned out that hemp was a relative of the marijuana plant, and it was used to make rope. The movie showed us all the hundreds of ways that rope, and thus hemp, was used in the war effort. The most startling example was a ship's anchor rope that was twenty-four inches in circumference. Just imagine a rope that was twenty-four inches in circumference!

As the movie ended, the county agent had a few things to add. He said, "As we speak, a hemp factory is being built in Union Grove, and they will take all the hemp you can produce. The price has not been determined, but I have been assured that it will be at a price surpassing what you would earn from corn or wheat. Plus, the government will provide the seed for free. One last thing, since hemp is a cousin to marijuana, anyone growing hemp must get a marijuana stamp, and I have the forms to get that stamp."

As we filed out, almost everyone picked up the form to apply for the marijuana stamp. Apparently, Yorkville farmers would be growing one hell of a lot of hemp.

So it began; I believe every farmer in Yorkville planted at least ten acres of hemp. As the summer proceeded, at every gathering, farmers would be talking about their hemp crop. They were so into hemp growing that they almost forgot to complain about the weather and the heat. Almost.

In May, the farmers were saying, "My hemp is over a foot tall." In June, the talk was "My hemp is more'n three feet tall." In late August, some farmers were bragging that their hemp was fourteen feet tall! Then came the harvest. To harvest hemp, you needed to cut it, let it dry for a few days, and then load it onto a wagon and take it to the hemp mill in Union Grove. As the first load arrived at the hemp mill, a mighty cry reverberated through Yorkville. "They say my hemp is too big, they are only going to pay half what they would pay for eight-foot stalks." So all this time, farmers were trying to grow the tallest hemp, and it turned out the shorter hemp produced the most profit! Luckily for me, I had planted the hemp on some old clay hills because I was suspicious of how profitable this crop would be. Being on clay hills, the crop grew to what turned out to be the perfect height and produced a tidy profit.

As the war came to a close, between Ann's work at Twin Disc, the extra land I rented, and the tremendous increase in farm prices, Ann and I had a tidy sum of money. What to do? We could use a new car, but they were still rationed and unavailable. Same with a new tractor. Maybe this would be the time to give Mom and Dad an ultimatum. Either I became a full partner in the farm or Ann and I would go off on our own.

Ann and I discussed this at length. Ann couldn't see me sacrificing everything for the farm and still just be a hired man. She made it clear that the loss of time with her and our son just wasn't worth it.

I've tried to put myself in Mom and Dad's shoes. I was sure Dad enjoyed the power of making the decisions. But the more I thought of it, the power to make decisions on a farm could be a curse. Was the weather right for planting? For haying? Should we harvest now or wait for the grain to dry further? Each of these decisions could make a tremendous difference in the prosperity of the farm. I would think Dad would value having someone to share the burden of those decisions.

That leaves only one possibility—Mom. Mom wanted to be in control. It was not so much, I thought, that I would be an equal partner. I thought it was that in some ways Ann would be equal in stature to her. Could that be it? Was that the reason I was still a hired man here? Or was it something more? Here I was, thirty-two years old, and I had never really stood up to my mom. Now was the time!

BOOK THREE

John Foxwell

CHAPTER ONE

First Memories

M Y MEMORY IS very clear of the full manure spreader being pulled by two seemingly humongous draft horses. I remember being lifted to the seat of the spreader. I was wearing a winter coat, and I think I was three. I don't remember who lifted me, but I can see and feel my grandfather, Tom Foxwell, Sr., wrapping his arms around me. As I settled into his lap, I can still see and hear him give a command to the horses. He contorted the right side of his face and gave a sound, using the clicking of his tongue and away we went. Starting with this ride, a bond was established between me and my grandfather that has never been broken.

My second memory is nothing like the first, and it embarrasses me to tell it. I was probably closer to my fourth year. I was looking at the Sears catalog, and I liked the pictures of the scantily clad women. I liked them so much that I began to cut them out with scissors. When my mother saw what I was doing, she slapped my hand and told me I was doing a bad, bad thing. I began to see that life was going to be more complicated than I realized. I always knew my mom and dad loved me, but it seemed they had a clear line between right and wrong. A line that, at least for a four-year-old, was sometimes difficult to see.

I don't want you to get the wrong idea about my mom. I always knew she loved me. Probably the best example would be how she took care of me when I was sick. It was like being a prince! She would check on me at least every fifteen minutes and inquire what I needed. If I wanted juice, it would be there. If I wanted toast, it would be there. Whatever I wanted, it would be delivered posthaste. If truth be told, I faked being sick a few times simply to feel loved.

My dad also loved me, but in a very different way. He was always so busy with farmwork that I often felt like an afterthought. I loved it when he would take me with him to get parts at the Allis Chalmers dealer or feed at the mill. I think the following two examples would give you a picture of our relationship.

The winter of my fourth birthday, we had a blizzard, and the drifts were way, way over my head. Dad said, "Come on outside, and we'll dig a tunnel under one of the drifts." I was in heaven to be with my dad and to have my first snow tunnel. We dug, or should I say Dad dug, for a good period of time. First, he would dig from one side of the drift and then from the other side, hoping that the two tunnels would meet in the middle. Just as he was about to break through, he said, "Chore time, I gotta go." I was crushed.

Another time, he and Grandpa spent the day building a new woven wire fence to keep the cows in the pasture. I was allowed to sit atop an overlooking hill in the old Chevy pickup. Sometimes I slept. Sometimes I watched. Sometimes I fooled around with the controls on the pickup. As the day was about over, I wondered what the big lever on the floor did. Before I knew it, I was rapidly gaining speed as I careened down the hill right through the brand-new fence. The next thing I knew, Dad was opening the door, and I thought he was going to hit me. Instead he got kind of a crooked smile on his face and just said, "You all right?" How did a four-year-old know what the reaction was going to be? Like I said before, life was complicated.

Most of the rest of my childhood memories revolve around my grandfather. The two of us would get on my horse, Tippy, and away we would go. The last words before our adventure were always the same. Grandpa would yell, "Zeno the Australian Snake Eater!" He never fully explained why or what that was about, but I knew it meant something special to him. One of our horseback adventures was to a nearby abandoned gravel pit. The gravel pit had been used for generations to provide gravel for the cement needed for barn and house foundations, silos, and road construction. I'm not really sure who it belonged to. It was sure not your average gravel pit; it was at least forty acres and overrun with trees and bushes. It was so thick that it was difficult to walk through. We dismounted, tied Tippy to a tree, and explored on foot. We found somewhere between six and eight huge animal holes. Some of them were big enough that I could have crawled right in, if I was brave enough (which I was not). We imagined mink, lions, tigers, or bears living in these holes. We convinced ourselves that we could

JAMES R. VYVYAN SR.

make our fortune trapping some of these animals. So on our next trip, we decided to bring a big steel trap, the kind that would snap shut on the unsuspecting animal.

We continued exploring and came across a shack. Even calling it a shack gave it more credit than it was due. It was made of two or three old doors, a couple of sheets of plywood, and some scrap lumber.

"Does someone live here?" I asked.

"I have no idea." We poked around the shack and found evidence of a fire and some empty soup cans. Grandpa got a kind of worried look on his face as he spoke, "Either someone is living back here or some kids are using this as a playhouse."

The next day, we returned, and Grandpa set the trap and staked it down. I covered it with a little grass to hide it. We also went back to the shack. The fire pit was warm. It looked more and more like someone was living there.

"This is kind of creepy."

Grandpa responded, "Let's keep our wits about us and tell your dad when we get back."

We rode Tippy back to the house, and I sprinted to tell Dad about what we had found.

"Dad, someone's living in the gravel pit!"

"Are you sure?"

Grandpa jumped in. "Sure does look like it. We were there yesterday and the fire pit was cold, and today it was still warm from a fire."

"We better keep our valuables locked up. No telling what kind of person is back there."

I could barely wait until the next day so we could check our trap and the shack. As soon as we finished chores, I started begging Grandpa to saddle up. I noticed Grandpa did something he had never done before. He strapped a big wooden club to the saddle. Now I was really excited. Was the club for the animal or the person living back there? When we got to the gravel pit, I ran to the trap. There it was! A huge groundhog was caught in the trap and struggling to be free. Grandpa caught up to me, and we gave each other a look that said, "Oh god, what have we done!" Grandpa sent me back to Tippy to get some gloves, but I think that was just a ruse to get me out of sight. When I returned, the groundhog was dead, and the club was in Grandpa's hand. We never ever mentioned trapping again. We did go farther into the pit to check on the shack. The fire pit was cold, but I noticed Grandpa kept the club by his side as we approached.

Our other adventures were far more fun and less scary than the one just described. In Yorkville, there seemed to be an abundance of bachelor farmers. I have no idea why, there just was. Grandpa felt it was his duty and pleasure to visit them on a regular schedule. Often he would take me along.

My favorite such visit was to Sam Owens' place. Sam was about Grandpa's age, and he lived alone in an old farmhouse. As we knocked on the door, Sam answered, dressed in clothes Grandpa later described as humble patches. We were escorted into the kitchen, and we noticed that Sam was limping.

Grandpa queried, "What happened to your leg?"

"Oh, it's nothing."

"Looks like it hurts pretty bad."

"Oh, all right, I'll tell you the story. Ya see, I have a real problem with rats. They love my corncrib, but when it gets real cold, they find a way into the house. So on a cold winter night, I'll lay in bed with my 22. Soon as I see a rat, I blast it. Except, one night, I missed the rat and got my big toe."

I tried to hide the smile and shock on my face, but I'm sure I failed. He shot his big toe while lying in bed; I couldn't believe it.

However, the big toe was only part of Sam's story. As we were sitting around the kitchen table, I noticed a hole in the floor. It was more than a foot long and about four inches wide. My curiosity got the best of me.

"What's the hole for?" as I pointed toward the hole.

"Well, when I sweep the floor, I just sweep the dirt right into the hole. It saves a lot of time."

"But where does it go?"

"Just into the basement."

I couldn't even imagine what the basement must look like, but I didn't pursue the subject.

On another such visit, we stopped at Frank Buchman's place. It was a brick house even older and more dilapidated than Sam's. Frank was much older than Grandpa. He walked all stooped over and had a long gray beard. Frank and Grandpa got to talking about the old days. They talked about the threshing bees and harvesting ice from the ponds. Meanwhile, I looked around the kitchen. He apparently lived in this one room because his bed was in the corner. I quietly went over and sat on the edge of the bed. My purpose was to explore the large number of blankets on the bed. I counted five blankets below the sheets and six blankets on top. I later asked Grandpa about it. He explained that the only heat he had was the stove in the kitchen, and on a cold winter night, it might get below freezing in the kitchen. Grandpa said that's the way all the houses were when he was growing up. The idea just made me shiver.

I feel a need to tell you one more bachelor farmer story. This story concerns hybrid seed corn. I was only six, but I was a good listener, and I knew a lot about hybrid seed corn. A man named Wallace started the Pioneer Seed Corn Company before I was born, and they produced the first hybrid seed corn. Dad explained it to me like this: "With cows, you breed a cow with weak front legs to a bull with strong front legs, and then hopefully, the result is a calf with the best features of both." I also knew that people didn't marry relatives because the babies could be weak or deformed. Dad said, "Using corn from the crib for seed the following year is like marrying your sister." Anyway, all the farmers Dad talked to were using hybrid seed and the yields jumped significantly.

So Grandpa and I visited Kenny. I don't know his last name. We found him in the corncrib shelling cob corn by hand.

Grandpa spoke first, "What ya doin, Kenny?"

"I'm getting some seed for planting. I'm real careful about taking the seed only from the big cobs so I get a good yield."

Grandpa knew, and I knew, that was a bunch of hooey. At this point, I'm wondering, *Will Grandpa let him know how wrong he is?* Grandpa was not that kind of a guy. He could have told Kenny how foolish he was, but he didn't. If Kenny had asked for advice, Grandpa would have been right there, but Grandpa was not the kind to make someone feel foolish.

One last thing about Grandpa. We covered for each other. If I made a mistake, he would find a way to keep it from Dad. If he made a mistake, I would do my best to keep Dad from finding out. Here's an example: It was a dry year, and we didn't have enough hay for the winter. Dad and Grandpa found a field of hay near Racine and purchased the standing hay. So they had to cut the hay, rake the hay, bale the hay, and haul it home. Everything went fine until Grandpa and I were hauling the hay home. It was a hot summer day, and we had the windows down. Grandpa was driving the old Chevy pickup pulling the big load of hay, and I was sitting next to him. To get home, we had to go up and over an overpass. Looking back, Grandpa should have started in a lower gear, because two thirds of the way up the overpass, the engine started turning slower and slower. I began to think, *I hope we can, I hope we can, I hope we can.* Just as we were about to reach the top of the overpass, the engine killed. Grandpa pushed the clutch in to restart the engine, except that as he pushed the clutch in, we started rolling back down the hill. Imagine not just the truck rolling backward but the big load of hay too. Cars started beeping, people started swearing. Then the sickening sound of the load of hay hitting one of the cars behind us. I was scared.

A big, big man came to the driver's side window. "What the hell are you doing?"

Grandpa remained calm and said, "What will it take to make things right?"

"Three hundred bucks."

Grandpa took out his checkbook and wrote the check. We started back up the overpass, except this time in a lower gear. Grandpa knew I would never tell Dad or Grandma, and I never did.

There is another memory that has left a deep and lasting impression on me. I was probably close to six years old and playing by myself as usual. I thought I would practice my croquet skills so I could beat my parents or grandparents. As you probably know, in croquet, if you hit an opponent's ball, you get to send that ball as far as you can. I was practicing just such a move, and apparently, I had perfected the move, because the ball went clear across the lawn and into the pasture. I carelessly went running after it and ducked under the electric fence. The next thing I knew, I was flying through the air. I hadn't realized that our big bull, General, was in the pasture. (Dad said General was an ornery SOB and that he weighed close to a ton.) After I came down, General started rolling me across the grass with his head. Luckily, I was able to roll right under the electric fence. I came up bleeding from my nose, and my clothes were ripped and nearly torn off. I ran as fast as I could to Mom. Later, I heard Mom and Dad having a serious talk about what happened. At that time, I didn't have a very well-developed sense of life and death. However, since that time, I've often thought about how close I came to death. Farms are dangerous places.

One last memory: It was the year I turned five. Christmastime was at hand, and the talk of the town was more about Pearl Harbor than it was about Christmas. On Christmas Eve, we had a gathering at our house, or should I say our side of the house, since we shared the house with Grandpa and Grandma Foxwell. The gathering included my grandparents; the Hansons; Mom's sister, Gloria; her husband, Jim; and their daughter, Carol.

It was unusual to have the family gathering on Christmas Eve. Normally, we would go to the ceremony put on by the English Settlement Church. Every Christmas Eve, they had a ceremony in a local barn. There would be baby Jesus in a real manger with hay and everything. He would be surrounded by Mary and Joseph. Everybody claimed that at the stroke of midnight, all the animals in the barn would lie down and be especially quiet as we sang "It Came upon a Midnight Clear." The adults claimed that the animals knew that this was the time of Jesus's birth. I've always had my doubts.

Anyway, back to the gathering at our house. Along about midnight, there was a knock on the front door. I ran to answer it, and lo and behold, it was Santa! He picked me up in his arms and said, "Merry Christmas! Merry Christmas! Have you been a good little boy?" I assured him that I was, and he pulled a big box out of his bag. I instantly ripped off the wrapping paper, and there was a new Lionel train! But to my chagrin, I was so busy with the train that I forgot to watch Santa leave. Here was my one chance to prove that Santa was real, and I forgot to watch him leave! Were there reindeer and a sleigh out there? I'll never know, and this bothered me for years to come.

The next morning, I woke up early, and sure enough, there was another present under the tree and the name tag read, "From Mom and Dad." I started to rip it open, but Mom jumped in. "Wait till your dad is done with chores." The next three hours were torture. Finally, Dad finished the chores and came in for breakfast. Only then was I permitted to open the gift. It turned out to be a Barber-Greene conveyor with a belt that you could move with a crank. I spent the day trying to elevate everything I could think of—kernels of corn, nuts, and even some cranberries.

After I opened my present, Mom opened her present from Dad. It was strange because when she unwrapped it, she got the funniest look on her face. Then she spoke quietly and softly, "Tom, it's the same exact sweater you got for me last Christmas."

"When I saw it, I knew instantly that I liked it. Now I know why!"

Except for missing Santa leave, it was a good Christmas.

CHAPTER TWO

Grandpa Tom

PLOWING A FIELD can be a mindless job. Our Allis Chalmers WC pulls a 2-16 plow. This means, each time I go across the field, I turn over a swath thirty-two inches wide. Today, I was plowing a field about a thousand feet wide. You get the idea. It gives a lot of time for a mind to wander. I'm approaching sixty years of age, and there's a lot of stuff stored in my old noggin.

One of the images that pass through my mind is a picture of Linda. God, how I loved that girl! It still turns my stomach when I think of how it ended. Where would I be today if we had married? I've tried to rationalize the situation in every way I know how. You can't be swept off your feet forever. Sooner or later, you come down to everyday life. You work, you talk, you eat, you sleep, and the next day, you do it all over again. Would it have worked for us? My mind has looked at this from a thousand different angles, and I still don't know. What I'd give to forget all about her.

Sometimes pictures of my wife, Grace, float through my mind. We'd started out at such a high; I should have known it couldn't stay that way. Over the last thirty years, every argument, every harsh word has put one more brick in the wall between us. Now I don't think either one of us could scale that wall. Too much has passed. I can't blame it all on her. No marriage fails with one party 100 percent at fault and the other innocent. Yet I would give anything for some real warmth between us. What can we do? We both know that we'll just keep on keeping on. I'll keep milking the cows, tending the crops, and Grace will continue cooking, cleaning, and washing. It's a hard way to live.

My mind often turns to Tom Jr. He's a good man, good son, and a hard worker. I couldn't ask for more. Today, I've decided it's time. I'm nearly sixty, and Tom Jr. is nearly thirty, a husband, and a father, yet he continues to work as a hired man. It's just not right. He's our only son. Up until this time, Grace has always tried to stop the transfer of half the farm to Tom. No more! I've only stood up to Grace on a couple of occasions; this will be another. I dread the argument we're going to have, yet I know I can't force her to sign the transfer papers. She refuses to explain herself except to say, "It's not the right time."

Thoughts of Tom Jr. lead to thoughts of his wife, Ann. She's a peach. Ann is prettier than a golden field of wheat ready to harvest. Any man would be proud to have Ann for a wife. In many ways, I envy the relationship my son and Ann have. She's not only pretty, but she's also honest, polite, loving, and pretty much the perfect wife for a farmer. If I hurt myself working on the farm, I always go to Ann to clean up the wound and put on a bandage. It's not only that she's good at it, but she's also so full of sympathy and caring for her old father-in-law. I love her as a daughter.

You'd think that as my mind wanders, pictures of my son Joe would turn up. Those pictures are buried so deep that only when I'm feeling especially strong do I bring them up. When I do, the picture of Joe lying dead at the bottom of the silo is on top. Grace and I have never been ourselves since Joe died. Something went out of us. I know I have had no desire to work, or anything else, in the twenty years since Joe died.

But then something totally unexpected happened, my grandson, John. It's almost like John has filled the hole in my heart left by Joe's death. When I'm with John, it's almost like he is my missing son. John is such a joy, and I know he feels the same way about me. Our time together is such a blessing!

A simple example would be when we pod peas. His mother, Ann, usually picks the peas, and John and I shuck the peas. We'll take a seat under the big maple trees and have a game to see who can find the pod with the most peas. To see the joy in his face when he finds a pod with twelve peas in it is really special. As he starts to tire of the job, I'll say, "You know what you need?"

"No, what do I need?"

"You need a black cow."

Then his blue eyes will get big and a smile will fill his face. A few minutes later, I'll return with a mixture of root beer and vanilla ice cream. We'll take a break from the peas and talk about our next adventure. It might be a horseback ride, catching crabs or minnows from the canal, or a trip to the Rocket Inn. The Rocket Inn is a nearby restaurant that makes the biggest and best banana splits. John always says, "Grandpa, let's rocket inn and rocket out!"

Probably one of the proudest moments for John and me was when I harnessed one of our horses, hitched it to the sleigh, and went up to Yorkville School. I gave every student a ride, including the schoolteacher. We would go around the school yard and then down the road a piece and back. I know that day, John felt like one lucky boy to have me for a grandfather.

Once in a while, John will get into a little trouble. He knows I'll do what I can to help him out. A good example would be the phone call yesterday. Mrs. Gorzky called, looking for John's dad or mom. I pretended to be John's dad because I knew she was up to something. She started, "Your son, John, has been picking on my son, and I want it stopped."

I just replied nicely, "I'll take care of it today."

Now, I knew there was no way John had been picking on the Gorzky boy, but I had a talk with John and made sure he knew to take a wide berth when it came to the Gorzkys.

One last thing about my grandson, John: he makes me laugh. I'll never forget the Easter Sunday when John was four. The five of us were coming home from church, and John ran ahead of us to the house. I didn't know then, but it was because he had left his dog, Blackie, in the house. Blackie, a nearly grown dog of unknown heritage, was an outdoor dog and was not to be left alone in the house. As we got to the house, a blue-eyed, blond-haired four-year-old was standing at the kitchen door with his little arms spread across the door frame.

"Mommy, you can't go in there!"

"Why, Johnny, you know I have to get in the kitchen and start working on Easter dinner."

"Don't go in there, Mommy!"

Of course, now we all had to go into the kitchen. Ann had left the ham on the kitchen counter. Now there was a huge, greasy streak where Blackie had pushed the ham across the kitchen floor. All that was left was the bone that Blackie was chewing contentedly.

CHAPTER THREE

Baling Hay

I T WAS A beautiful June day, and I was midway through my sixth year. The day started out like any other day. Dad and Grandpa milked the cows, and I did my chores. My chores included feeding all the calves, scraping the manure into the gutters, and cleaning out the horse stalls.

I think it would be clearer if I described the dairy barn. The barn is about eighty feet long and thirty-five feet wide. The barn has two stories with the upper floor, the hay mow, used for storing hay. There are close to a dozen windows covered with steel bars on the first floor. Early on, I asked Dad, "Why are there bars on the windows?"

"Without them, the damn cows or horses have a habit of breaking the windows."

That made sense. There are four doors, a large six-foot door to the east and smaller doors on each of the other three sides. The first things you see as you walk in are two large horse stalls. One of my jobs is to clean out the horse manure each day. That's pretty easy. After the horse stalls, there are two more stalls that we keep cows in that are about to have calf. After birth, we keep the new calves in those stalls, and it's my job to feed the calves. This is also pretty easy except sometimes I have to let the calves suck on my fingers to help them learn how to drink from a pail. I hate that; it just feels so creepy. Finally, there are about thirty stanchions for the milk cows. After the cows leave the barn for pasture, I scrape the manure into the gutters. This is not my favorite job.

After breakfast, Dad announced that today we were going to bale hay. This meant that we would attach the WC to the baler. Grandpa usually drove the baler, and Dad would load the bales onto the wagon. I like to ride on the wagon with Dad. It was fun to be with Dad and Grandpa, and I also liked the way Dad piled the bales. He arranged them neatly like he was laying bricks. He told me if he didn't do it just right, the bales would likely fall off the wagon.

Usually we hired a couple of high school boys to take the full wagons back to the barn and pile the bales in the haymow. I noticed that if things were going well, we would pay them a dollar an hour; if not, it was fifty cents per hour.

Today things were not going well. One of the boys decided not to come at the last moment. This was a big problem. Workers were hard to find. The war was on, and workers were scarce. Dad and Grandpa talked for a while, and finally Dad said to me, "We need you to drive the tractor and baler."

I had never driven a tractor in my life. I was only six. I was a little scared. Dad explained how to use the foot clutch, turn on the power take-off, and shift gears. The biggest problem was that, since I was so small, in order to put the foot clutch in, I had to get off the seat of the tractor and sit on the floor of the tractor, bracing my back against the seat.

Off we went. I made a few rounds, and things were going great. I fell in love with driving a tractor. I was doing a man's work at the age of six. I was pretty proud. Then it happened. I got a little too far from the windrow of hay and the baler plugged up. I got off the seat, sat on the floor of the tractor, and pushed the clutch in. Dad got off the wagon and came around to unplug the baler. This is when I realized that if my foot slipped off the clutch, Dad could be killed. That's a pretty sobering thought for a six-year-old! But my foot didn't slip off the clutch, Dad got the baler unplugged, and away we went.

In fact, the day went great. I was so, so proud. I couldn't wait to tell Mom that I had done a man's work. I slept soundly that night and dreamed about tractors and being a man.

CHAPTER FOUR

The Accident

S O IT WENT that summer. I drove the baler and was proud of it. Some say that pride goes before the fall. I don't know about that. All I know is that I continued to drive the baler, and my parents like to brag about it to their friends. I did notice that some of their friends seemed quite shocked that I was driving a baler at the age of six—six and a half really.

It was near the end of summer, and we were baling wheat straw. It was what my parents referred to as the dog days of August. It was miserably hot. The windrows were big and damp because of the dew and humidity. The straw didn't feed into the baler worth a damn. I was constantly stopping and letting Dad unplug the baler while I held the clutch in.

The baler has a pickup, auger, and a plunger. The pickup does what it says; it picks up the straw and feeds it into the auger. The auger moves the hay or straw toward the bale chamber that contains the plunger. The plunger is a big rectangular object with a sharp knife that cuts the hay or straw. The plunger goes back and forth, packing the hay into a bale and cutting the stems of the material for a nice rectangular bale.

Anyway, on this day, the straw seemed to get stuck right at the point where the straw was going into the bale chamber. So when I stopped the baler, Dad would reach in and push the straw into the bale chamber. Except this time, when I stopped and Dad reached in, a big nasty wasp stung me right on the cheek. I instantly jumped, and my foot slipped off the clutch. There was a cry from my dad. I managed to get the clutch in and shut off the tractor. I looked back and Dad was holding an arm with no hand.

What have I done? What have I done? I felt nauseous and sick all over, and then I must have blacked out. The next thing I knew, I was lying in bed, and it was nighttime. Then a small sliver of hope came to me. Could this have been a dream? One terrible, terrible nightmare? No, it had to be real; it was too clear, too vivid, too sickening. Is there the slightest chance that this could have been a dream? I had to know for sure. I climbed out of bed and crept down the stairs. I could hear voices. I didn't let myself be seen, but I looked around the corner and Mom and Dad were at the kitchen table. Dad was sitting there, and *thank God, he had two hands!*

Soon, after the relief flowed through my body, I could tell they were having a serious discussion. Mom initiated, "Tom, we made good money on the two farms you rented, we have the money from my town job, and as you know, I recently received a small inheritance from my aunt. Tom, we could put a down payment on our own place. The Skewes place is for sale at a good price. We could have a house to ourselves." Dad was quiet for a good long time. Finally, he spoke, quietly and slowly, "These are the hardest words I've ever had to say. Ann, I can't do it. I love you as much as any man can love a woman, but I just can't leave this farm. I've lived here all my life. I was here when my brother died. I've put enough sweat into this place to fill a lake. When we put running water to the house, I dug a trench six feet deep and two hundred feet long to lay the pipe. I did this by hand. I was here when the tornado hit and we had to rebuild the barn. Every place I look, I see my sweat. I'm the one who paid off the mortgage and saved the farm from auction. I'm the one who has kept this farm moving. My dad hasn't been worth a darn since Joe died. It's all been me. I can't give all this up."

Mom slumped in her chair, and tears trickled down her cheek. "You mean I'll have to live in these three rooms for the rest of my life? Living with a woman, your mom, who treats me like dirt." Dad didn't respond.

CHAPTER FIVE

To Turn the Earth

IT WAS A comfortable August morning. Yesterday we spent the day baling second-crop hay. This morning, Dad said something that surprised me, "I want you to take the WC and plow the wheat field." Now I've ridden with Dad or Grandpa many times as they plowed a field, but I've never been allowed to do this job by myself. I've been driving the baler for four years, but Dad has always been on the wagon behind me.

Let me explain plowing. The Allis Chalmers WC pulls a 2-16 plow. This means that it takes two ribbons of soil, sixteen inches wide and six inches deep, and turns those strips upside down. As you can imagine, this process takes a lot of power; it really makes the WC snort. Sometimes, especially going up a clay hill, the WC will be pulling so hard that the front wheels will come clear off the ground!

I checked the oil, filled it with gas, and Dad helped me hook up the plow. The wheat field was a quarter mile east of the farm buildings. As I approached the field, I began to ponder the job at hand. Farmers take pride in their plowing. One of the key things is that the ribbon of soil, called a furrow, be as straight as a pin. Since this field was visible from the road, I had to be extra careful; otherwise, the result would be an embarrassment to Dad and Grandpa.

The field was about a half mile long. This means I would have to pull the rope, which drops the plow into the ground, and travel 2,500 feet without even a wiggle. I dropped the plow and aimed for a big tree at the far end of the field. I resisted the temptation to look back, because I might inadvertently turn the steering wheel. Finally, I got to the other end of the field, pulled the rope to raise the plow, stopped the tractor, and took time to look back. It wasn't perfect, there was a little curve in the furrow, but acceptable for a first try.

As the morning continued, I went up and back, up and back, over and over again. Each time I went across the field, another thirty two inches would be plowed. I started to relax and enjoy the day. The first thing I noticed was the sweet smell of the soil. I once mentioned to a friend that I liked the smell of the soil. He was incredulous. "You like the smell of dirt?" I let the subject drop, but really, if the soil is rich in organic matter, I love the aroma.

The second thing I noticed was the birds. We often go for months and never see a seagull; after all, we are twenty miles from Lake Michigan. However, drop the plow in the ground and within a half hour, hundreds of seagulls will appear. I don't know how they do it. Do they smell the rich soil? I don't know. What I do know is they appear to be having a picnic. All the worms and grubs that are exposed as the soil is turned seem to be like an exotic dessert to the seagulls. Plus, they get incredibly bold. The WC is moving about two miles per hour. The birds will walk within a foot or two of the plow. There seems to be some kind of contest to get the freshest worms from the newly turned soil.

Then things took a turn for the worse. I heard a thump and felt the tractor jerk. The plow had run into a big stone. The plow is equipped with a special spring loaded hitch. The purpose of this hitch is to unhook the plow, if it hits an obstruction. If the plow didn't detach from the tractor, something would have to give, probably the plow would bend or break. Now I have to find a way to reattach the plow to the tractor. This is no easy task when you're by yourself.

The strange thing is that the next time around, I hit the same stone at the same place. This happened five times in a row! This stone must be huge! At thirty-two inches per time, this stone must be more than thirteen feet wide! Just then Dad brought me lunch. "Dad, I've hit the same rock five times in a row!"

"I know, I know, I've hit that sucker each year for the last twenty years. I've had enough! I'm calling the Welch brothers to bring out a Caterpillar to dig that rock out once and for all!"

The Welch brothers arrived with a semi carrying an Allis Chalmers HD16. The thing was huge. Bill Welch said it weighed almost twenty tons. Bill spent about an hour exposing the rock. It turned out to be thirteen feet wide by twenty feet long and ten feet high! So now the rock was sitting in a huge hole totally exposed. Bill lined up the huge machine to push the rock out of the hole. He revved the powerful engine and engaged the transmission. The rock wouldn't move.

Bill and his brother, Ron, had a conference, and before I knew it, they had piled twenty pounds of dynamite on top of the stone. What were they going to do? They then covered the dynamite with several hundred pounds of clay, which they packed tightly. Bill told me to stay behind his truck. Ron counted down, ten, nine . . . two, one. *Kaboom!* The clay reached a height of at least fifty feet, but what had they accomplished? The rock was still there. Upon closer inspection, they had accomplished something. There was a crack; they had split the stone in two. Again they lined up the HD16, but this time only on half of the rock. They could make the rock wiggle but were unable to push even the half of the rock out of the hole.

They ended up bringing in a second HD16, and the two machines together were able to push each half up and out. Now we had two problems. What to do with the two rocks and what to do about the huge hole. It was decided to push the rocks to the canal bank, where they would never be hit by a plow again. Then they brought in an earthmover to fill the gigantic hole.

The following day, I returned to finish plowing. As I went round and round, I came closer and closer to the big hill. Most of our soil is a dark, sandy loam, but the hill is heavy, light-colored clay. As I got close to the hill, the tractor really had to work. It took every single horsepower to pull the plow through the clay. Then, all of a sudden, it was like plowing butter. A couple of seconds later, the tractor was again pulling for all it was worth. The next time around, the same thing happened, except this time the easy plowing continued for a little longer. This continued for about eight rounds, or about twenty feet of plowed ground. At this point, there was no easy plowing; it continued to be heavy clay all the way across the hill. I looked over to the area that plowed so easily, it was a dark color, not clay at all. What the heck? The top of the hill, if nothing else, should be a light-colored, heavy clay.

When I finished plowing, I approached Dad and Grandpa as they were cleaning the chicken house. "The plowing went well, except on the top of the big hill there was a spot that plowed like butter."

Grandpa got a strange look on his face. "Was that area slightly raised as compared to the surrounding clay soil?"

"Why, I hadn't thought about it, but it was somewhat raised in comparison to the surrounding clay."

Grandpa looked like he was hit by lightning. "Get some shovels, John."

Grandpa and I rode the WC back to the big hill. As we traveled, Grandpa explained. "As you know, my grandfather, your great-great-grandfather bought this farm from the government in the late 1830s. I have the deed in the house. Along with the deed are the notes of the original surveyor of the land. It's been a few years since I read those notes, but I remember seeing the words 'raised mound found in prairie.' You may have found that mound."

As we reached the big hill, just like I said, there was a dark circle of soil, and yes, it was about six to ten inches higher than the surrounding soil. Grandpa and I started to dig in the center of the dark soil. For the first eighteen inches, there was nothing, and then my shovel hit something. I shoveled further and picked up a piece of flat copper about two by three inches. I cleaned it off, and there was a rough drawing of a bird etched on the copper. I was beyond excited, and I could tell Grandpa was too. We dug farther, and this time, Grandpa struck something. It was obviously a point for a spear, and it was made out of a type of stone that I had never seen. Upon further digging, we hit one more thing, a bone. As we examined it, it was clearly a leg bone. Grandpa spoke first and solemnly, "This is an Indian cemetery."

Grandpa slowly and reverently put the three items back in the hole, and we filled the hole together. Grandpa continued, "We must never farm this area again, this is sacred ground."

I was full of questions. "Who built this mound? When was it built? Why was it built?"

Grandpa had no answers; he simply stated, "I'm glad to finally know what the surveyor was writing about, but I'm sad that we've disturbed this grave. I don't know how your father and I missed it all these years."

When I got back to school that fall, I told my teacher, Mr. Andersen, what we had found. Mr. Andersen was excited. "Wow! I wrote my master's thesis on Indian mounds. Let me fill you in." He was able to answer my questions. He told me that there are over one hundred such mounds in Racine County, and they were built about a thousand years ago. Originally, people thought they were built by a lost race. They thought this for three reasons: (1) They thought the Indians were savages and incapable of building such mounds. (2) They needed to think of the Indians as savages to justify the taking of their lands. (3) Since the Indians don't now build mounds, it was thought that they never did. Finally, he said the reason the mounds were built was likely because they believed in an afterlife and wanted to set the dead on that journey.

I've thought about that mound many, many times. To think that there were Indians living on our farm a thousand years ago is mind-numbing. The amount of work necessary to build such a mound is incredible. They must have carried the dirt, by hand, sack by sack. I have new respect for our farm, the soil, and the many generations that have preceded us.

JAMES R. VYVYAN SR.

CHAPTER SIX

Growing Up

I WENT TO the same one-room school as my dad and grandpa. I was almost always top in my class. Of course, there were only four students in my class. This included Bill Skewes, Patty Voss, Jon Gorzky, and me.

High school was a whole new ball game. The first step was signing up for classes. For the first time, I had a choice of what classes to take. It surprised me that I signed up for a course in agriculture. When had I decided to be a farmer? Or had I?

Even though the high school was in Union Grove, a town of only two thousand people, there was a tremendous separation between the farm boys and the townies. We farm boys were referred to as plow boys, a name that chafed just a bit. In an attempt to fit in, I joined the football team. I knew nothing about football. In my freshman year, I was in the game for all of one play. I was a defensive tackle, and at the snap of the ball, I just kept hitting the offensive tackle across from me. I paid no attention to the runner; it turned out that was the last time the coach let me play.

To make things worse, Jon Gorzky made a friend of George Johnson. George was a townie. The two of them seemed to take delight in tormenting me. They were both bigger than me and just plain mean. Early in my freshman year, I was doing my duty on the toilet in the boys' room. I heard someone or some people enter. I heard talking and the smell of cigarette smoke but couldn't quite make out what they were saying. As I left the stall, I was dismayed to see that it was Jon and George. Jon grabbed me and pushed me against the wall.

"What are you doing in here?"

"What do you think I'm doing?"

Then George grabbed me and held my arms while Jon gave me a couple of good ones to the stomach.

"In the future, stay out of our way!"

Funny but it was the two of them that stayed out of my way. I heard through the grapevine that the two of them were arrested for burning down nearby Summit Grade School! I never did see the two of them again. Thank God! How twisted do you have to be to burn down a grade school?

At home, Grandma and Grandpa had just purchased a TV set. This meant that I spent my evenings on the other side of the house watching TV with them. They were some of the first in Yorkville to have a TV. The three of us loved the *Milton Berle Show* and the *Jack Benny Program*. I think they paid as much for the TV as they had for their car, but it sure was worth it.

I had been showing 4-H steers at the county fair since I was ten. Dad and Grandpa gave me free feed for the work I did around the farm. At the end of the fair, the steer was sold, and I would get to keep the money. So at the age of sixteen, I had quite a pile of cash, at least for a sixteen-year-old. So I purchased my first car, a used 1948 Ford Coupe. It was red, with baby moon hubcaps, and the nicest car in the school parking lot. To make it extra cool, I ordered a rear-seat speaker with a fader control from JC Whitney. Boy, I loved that car! I would sing along with "Unforgettable" by Nat King Cole and "A Kiss to Build a Dream On" by Louis Armstrong. Things were pretty darn good!

To me this meant I was ready for dating. I asked Barbara Bush to go to the movies. Actually, I was too shy to ask her, so I passed her a note. She passed me a note back and said, "Yes." So Friday at six, I picked her up. Boy, was I nervous. The movie *African Queen* was playing at the Venetian in Racine. I had been to Racine, but I had never driven to Racine. The combination of my first trip to Racine and my first date was almost too much, but we made it. Sitting in the theater, I thought I really should try to put my arm around Barbara. Friends had told me the tried-and-true method was to pretend to stretch and then leave your right arm fall around the girl's shoulders. (They told me the right arm, always go right, they said.) Success! I was in teenage heaven, sitting in a movie with my arm around a girl! Then a problem cropped up. My arm went to sleep and started to hurt, but if I removed my arm, later I'd have to go through the same lame process to get it back there. I decided to tough it out, but the pain kept getting worse. When will this movie end? Oh yeah, the movie, I guess it was pretty good. I really couldn't pay much attention; my arm hurt too badly.

This is about the time that my relationship with my dad took a turn for the worse. I'll admit a good part of it was my fault. My mind was on girls, cars, and fun. I'd stay out too late and really wasn't good for much the next day. Dad and Mom had just bought me a new pair of expensive Florsheim leather shoes for church. I remember them well because we purchased them at a store in West Racine where they had a fluoroscope machine. With this machine, you could see right through the shoe to see how the shoe fit. The shoes were very expensive, and I begged for them. They had little doodads that hung down on each side of the shoe. I had never seen a pair like them. I felt they were very distinctive. However, later that day, in my girl-fogged mind, I put them on top of my car and drove off, never to see them again. Dad didn't talk to me for a week. Not talking to me was his usual punishment. It got pretty old when we worked side by side all week.

CHAPTER SEVEN

The Contest

GRANDPA CRIED TODAY. We shipped our two draft horses to the fox farm. The horses hadn't been worked for at least a year, and they were very old, but they were like family to Grandpa. They had foundered and every step they took seemed to send them streams of pain. It was the right decision, but a hard one for Grandpa.

I've loved tractors since my first day driving the baler. The sale of the horses left us with an Allis Chalmers WC and a John Deere A to do all the farmwork. Neither of these tractors had electric start, and cranking them by hand was a real bitch. Plus, it seemed like all the neighbors were getting bigger and better tractors than we had. One of our neighbors, Ken Meyers, had four new tractors and a new self-propelled combine. I was beyond jealous. I knew that Dad and Grandpa would never buy a new tractor, but I had some hope that we could get a bigger and better used one. So every trip to the machinery dealer raised my hopes. Today was one of those days. Dad and I went to R. A. Mayer, the local Allis Chalmers dealer, to get some parts for the old WC. To Dad's credit, he asked the salesman if they had any good used tractors. The three of us took a walk to the lot. There it was: an Allis Chalmers Model U with great paint, tires, and electric start! I said, "Dad, I love this tractor. It would be perfect for our farm!"

Dad said to the salesman, "We'll think about it."

Dad grabbed my arm and dragged me to our truck and threw me into the passenger seat. *"Don't you ever say you like a tractor in front of the salesman!* It ruins our whole bargaining position, and we're not going to be able to negotiate a good price."

Yes, things got off to a bad start, but I was not about to give up. I was quiet for a couple of days to let things cool off. Luckily, I had grabbed the specs on the model U from the dealer's brochure rack and now I studied them carefully. I planned my attack. Grandpa was going to be the easier of the two. Technically, he controlled all purchases, but he was beginning to let Dad have more say. Week one, I kept repeating how the Model U weighed 1,300 pounds more than the WC, and I'll bet we'd be able to pull a three-bottom plow instead of a two bottom. Week two, I concentrated on the engine, and my mantra was the Model U has 20 percent more horsepower than the WC and 111 more cubic inches. Week three, I concentrated on the ease of electric start and that the gas tank on the U was 60 percent bigger. I knew my tactics had to be handled delicately. If I said too much, it could queer the whole deal. So in the fourth week, I remained quiet on the subject. Apparently, Dad and Grandpa had been talking because, on the Monday of the fifth week, the dealer delivered the Model U! I was beyond happy and rather impressed that my efforts had paid off, especially after the way it started.

I'd be lying if I said I wanted this tractor just because it would make our farm more efficient. I'd be lying if I said I wanted this tractor just because I wanted to keep up with the neighbors. The biggest reason I wanted this tractor was because it would be something I could enter in the county fair pulling contest and have a real chance to win. In that regard, I started working on a plan to win the pulling contest.

But things took an interesting twist. It was about nine o'clock at night, and I was watching TV with Grandma and Grandpa as usual. Surprisingly, there was a knock on the door. I ran to the door, and standing there was Ken Meyers with a hangdog look on his face. Ken wasn't even thirty years old, and I considered him a friend, even if I was jealous of his machinery. Ken moaned, "I need your help."

"Of course, what can I do for you?"

Ken continued, "I'm a loser! I've really messed up this time. I was plowing the marsh with my new International W9, and I got too close to a wet spot and got stuck. I walked back to the farm, got my brother, and we went back with my new International W6 to pull the W9 out, and I got that stuck. We walked back and did the same thing with the Farmall M and Farmall H. With one last gasp, I brought my new self-propelled combine down to pull out the H, and I got the combine stuck. I was hoping you could help."

I went back to my side of the house and had a conversation with Dad. Dad kept saying, "You're just going to get our tractor stuck." I, however, looked at this as a great opportunity to prove the worth of our

Model U, and so off I went. As I put my coat on, Dad said something totally out of character, "Go for it!"

When I got to the marsh, I was glad I had brought along a couple of extra chains. With the extra chains, I was able to get to some higher and, therefore, drier ground to pull from. It took several hours, but I was able to pull all five machines out of the marsh. It was one proud day for me and the Model U!

I then returned to the drawing board to plan my victory at the pulling contest. I had been watching the county fair pulling contest since I was six. I'd been taking notes since I was ten. Now that I was sixteen, it was the first year I would be eligible to participate. It had been drilled into me that there were only two kinds of tractor pullers, cheaters and losers. I didn't intend to be either.

Studying my notes, I determined that there were usually about twenty tractors in the seven-thousand-pound class. I weighed the Model U at the feed mill, and it came in at 6,600 pounds. This meant I would have to add some weight. The dealer sells iron weights at about fifty cents a pound. I didn't have $200 to buy the four hundred needed pounds, so I made concrete weights. I made forms so that the resulting concrete weight would fit nicely on the tractor's platform. One problem solved, the U will weigh the same as the other nineteen tractors—seven thousand pounds.

The second problem was a little more difficult. The U was not a new tractor. The new tractors had more horsepower. For example, I knew from past history that I'd be pulling against an International W9, Minneapolis Moline G, and a John Deere G. All three of them had more horsepower than my U. What to do?

I thought about the pull itself. Each tractor is hooked to what is known as a stoneboat. A stoneboat is a wooden object, approximately six feet wide and ten feet long, made out of heavy, wooden planks. As the tractor moves forward, every ten feet, a man jumps on the stoneboat. This makes the stoneboat heavier and, therefore, harder to pull. Eventually the stoneboat gets so hard to pull that it stops the tractor. Whichever tractor pulls it the farthest is the winner.

I thought about this for a long time. How could I defeat tractors that were newer and had a lot more horsepower? The cheaters either add more weight to their tractor when no one is looking or do mysterious things to the engine to produce more horsepower. Both of these things were illegal in the seven-thousand-pound stock class. I was determined not to cheat, but I was okay with bending the rules a bit. Then it occurred to me. The pulling contest started with the three-thousand-pound class, then the five-thousand-pound class, and finally the big boys, the seven-thousand-pound class. This meant that at least fifty tractors had an opportunity to pull, and this would take hours. From past experience, I knew that later in the night, many of the men jumping on the stoneboat would get thirsty and go to the beer tent. So my advantage would be if I pulled later, there would be fewer men jumping on the stoneboat, and it would be easier to pull.

Pulling contest day. The pull was scheduled for 6:00 p.m., and we had to weigh and register our tractors by 4:00 p.m. As I was registering, they told me to pick a number from a hat to determine the order of the pull. The hat was just sitting on the table, and in it were twenty slips of paper folded in half. I kept on a conversation with the registrar as I strained my eyes at the semi-folded slips. There it was—number 20—and I grabbed it. I would be pulling last. Let's hope my supposed advantage pays off.

Later I noticed that the three tractors I was most worried about pulled first, fifth, and fifteenth. I watched nervously from the pits. First up was the International W9. It made a real nice pull and stopped at a distance of 212 feet. The Minneapolis Moline G pulled fifth and also had a nice pull of 217 feet. As I was watching, I noticed a few of the men jumping on the stoneboat were beginning to leave for the beer tent. Now the John Deere G, it had a super slow gear we called the creeper gear, and it moved at a snail's pace down the track. But it just wouldn't stop and ended up pulling 257 feet.

Finally, it was my turn, the final pull of the night. All eyes were on me and my perfectly waxed Model U as I backed up to the stoneboat. I knew I had to beat 257 feet, and I could see exactly where that was because there was a man well over 350 pounds that jumped on at that spot. Off I went, and the Model U began to snort. At about 220 feet, the front wheels came off the ground—it was pulling so hard. I now could only steer with the brakes. Okay, where is that big guy—*he's gone!* So there was no 350 pounder to jump on, and I continued for a pull of 271 feet and the victory! What a glorious feeling!

CHAPTER EIGHT

The Mystery

YESTERDAY WAS THE best day of my life. I, John Foxwell, had the grand champion steer, won the pulling contest with my dad's Allis Chalmers Model U, and word got back to me that the prettiest girl in Yorkville likes me. Life is good! (I didn't know it then, but it would be a long time before I felt this way again.)

It was 6:00 a.m., and the sun was rising, and it was time to help my Dad, Tom Foxwell Jr., with the milking. Yet something didn't feel right; maybe it was just me coming down to earth after yesterday's excitement. As I was walking toward the barn, the sky was growing darker, and there were storm clouds on the horizon.

"Hi, Dad, sure looks like we've got some ugly weather heading our way." Dad nodded. I turned on the radio. Except for the market reports, Dad hated the radio and what he called the newfangled music. I, on the other hand, couldn't wait to hear my favorite song, "Please Send Me Someone to Love" by Percy Mayfield. That was not to be. What we heard was a news flash—President Truman had sent troops into Korea. Holy shit, I was only two years away from being eligible for the draft!

We milked the twenty-nine cows in silence. Dad wasn't much of a talker, at least not with me. The only sound was the rhythmic *click*, *click* of the milking machines.

As we finished milking, I thought, where was my dog Blackie? I had raised Blackie from a pup, and for the last ten years, he was the first to greet me as I walked to the barn. I left the barn and took a quick right to his doghouse. As I approached, I saw a trail of blood. Blackie lay dead at the door to his house; someone or something had ripped open his stomach. Through my tears, it dawned on me that last year the same thing happened to our best calf.

By this time, Dad and Grandpa had gathered around. Dad spoke first, "Once is enough, but twice is too much. I'm calling the vet to investigate."

Later that day, the vet arrived and spent time probing the wound. "I can't say for sure. It could be the claw of a big dog, cat, or a bear. It also could be the result of a dull knife. Can't say for sure."

Next, Dad called the police, and officer Bill Vivian responded. He also looked at the wound and looked around for tracks. The doghouse was just off the driveway, which was hard-packed gravel. There didn't seem to be any tracks. The only tracks visible probably resulted from Dad, Grandpa, the vet, and me. Officer Vivian asked us for our opinion on what happened.

Grandpa spoke first, "I think there is someone living in the gravel pit, and he might be responsible."

I chimed in, "We've also seen huge holes over at the gravel pit. I think a large cat or a bear could easily fit into them."

Officer Vivian asked if we've had any arguments with the neighbors.

Dad answered this one. "I think we get along with just about everybody. I can't think of anyone that's upset with us."

Vivian finished with, "I'll let you know if anything turns up."

I spent the rest of the day digging a grave for Blackie. I also constructed a cross out of some old snow fence slats. On the cross, I wrote, "Blackie—the best dog in the world." I was too upset to place Blackie in the grave, and Dad took over the rest of the job. I saddled up and went for a ride. I took along a couple of cans of soup. I rode back to the gravel pit, and the holes were as big as or bigger than ever. It was still unclear whether anyone lived in the shack. I left the cans of soup next to the shack. I returned the next day, and the soup cans were gone.

I told Mom and Dad I wanted to go back to the gravel pit at night and lie and wait for the man or beast that might have killed Blackie.

Dad responded first. "You will do no such thing! As overgrown as the gravel pit is, it's dangerous in the daytime and much worse at night." Mom just nodded in agreement.

Teenage boys are not known for listening to their parents, and the next night, I snuck out about 11:30 p.m., saddled Tippy, and grabbed the 12-gauge shotgun. I tied Tippy at the edge of the pit and worked my way in. There was about two thirds of a moon, and it was a clear night. I could see well enough. I was shocked to see that the shack was gone. Every board, every post, everything was gone! I found a high spot near there and lay with my shotgun at the ready. I hate to admit it, but I soon fell asleep. I awoke just as the sun was starting to light up the eastern sky. I rushed to get home before my parents woke up. As I reached Tippy, to my surprise, an old cloth flour sack was tied to the saddle horn. It was filled with a bunch of arrowheads and one spear point. What the hell?

A couple of weeks later, Mom and Dad gave me a new golden retriever puppy that I named Trooper. Every time I looked at Trooper, I thought of Blackie, but Trooper sure was cute, and it was like his sole aim in life was to please me. I never told anyone about the arrowheads or the missing shack. If I told my parents, they would know I snuck out. I didn't know what to do.

CHAPTER NINE

The Cold War

DECEMBER 1, 1950, will be a day that neither my parents nor I will ever forget. However, to tell the story, I need to start at the beginning. It all began years earlier as I listened to the *Captain Midnight* radio show. I loved the show. It had real mysteries that I so loved. However, to really understand the show, Captain Midnight told his listeners that they needed his secret decoder ring.

To get the ring, I needed to send in the top of an Ovaltine jar. Captain Midnight promoted Ovaltine by saying, "Drink Ovaltine if you want rocket power!" I would have to work on Mom to buy a jar, plus who doesn't want to have rocket power? "Mom, would you buy a jar of Ovaltine?"

"You don't like chocolate milk. It'll go to waste!"

"I'll drink it! I'll drink it!"

I got the Ovaltine and the secret decoder ring. Mom was right, I hated the Ovaltine, but I drank it.

At the end of each show, Captain Midnight gave a code telling about next week's episode. He might say, "For next week, the clue is 24-18-8-11-24-0-1-15-17-16-5-0-26-24." Using the secret decoder ring, I was able to figure out that the numbers stood for "spies among us." This is what got me started. I loved the idea of being able to read and write messages that only a few special people could understand. A couple of friends in school had the decoder rings too. We would send notes back and forth, knowing our teacher would never know what we were saying. That turned out to be not quite true. I didn't know that our teacher had a ten-year-old son. Nor did I know that the ten-year-old son had a decoder ring. I was glad the intercepted note only said she was boring. It could have been much worse.

The radio show and the decoder ring got me thinking about real spies and espionage. The Berlin Airlift was in all the newspapers. The commies had shut all the entrances to Berlin, and the Allies flew in all the needed food and supplies until the commies buckled. Just when we were feeling the joy of the commies buckling, they exploded their first atomic bomb. On another front, Mao Zedong had just completed his takeover of China. Plus, North Korea had invaded South Korea. Everyone was talking about whether the commies were going to take over the world.

As I was doing mindless farm chores, like forking the manure out of the calf pens, my mind would play out scenarios of Americans outmaneuvering the commies. In my mind, the Americans always won, but it was always close. I heard talk at the grocery store about communists infiltrating our country and how we should be on the lookout for commies even in Yorkville.

As I entered high school, I finally had access to a library. I quickly fell in love with an author by the name of Eric Ambler. Ambler seemed to have a real knack in writing mysteries, especially those involving spies. I read *Journey into Fear* and *Epitaph for a Spy*. I loved the way he wrote; in some cases, his mind and mine almost worked in unison. I could often predict what he was going to say next. I begged our librarian, Ms. Duckey, to get more Ambler books.

As mesmerized by mysteries and spy novels as I was, something I found stunned me. I was helping Mom clean out the storage room next to my bedroom, when I came across a Hardy Boys novel. The book was obviously well read; the pages were worn and dog-eared. But the thing that stunned me was the plaque on page 1 that said, "This book belongs to Tom Foxwell Jr." This was my dad's book! I never knew Dad to read a book. Plus, he apparently likes or liked the same type of books that I did. Why didn't he ever mention it? He's watched me reading similar books dozens of times. I don't understand.

The date is December 1, 1950. My car was in the shop getting a valve job. I was shoveling snow from the sidewalk and making paths to all the outbuildings. Grandma and Grandpa had gone Christmas shopping. Mom and Dad were visiting her parents. Then it happened, I heard the roar of a jet plane. Jets passing overhead were a new phenomena, and it excited me. Just last year, the Milwaukee 128th Fighter Squadron was one of the first in the nation to get the new Lockheed F80 Shooting Stars. Suddenly, smoke started streaming out of the plane, and it started to drop like a stone! At first, I thought it was going to fall right on our farm, but at the last minute, I could see it would fall slightly to the southeast of the farm.

I immediately jumped on the only vehicle available, my bike, and made a beeline for the smoke. As I pedaled wildly, I wondered if the plane had been shot down by the commies. Were we under attack? The wreckage was less than two miles from home, and I was one of the first on the scene. It was hard to believe the amount of wreckage that was spread over several acres. Where was the pilot? Did he parachute to safety?

More and more people arrived, and we did an impromptu search for the pilot. Our only hope was that he had parachuted to safety. No such luck, we eventually found the remains of the pilot trapped in the wreckage. Meanwhile I kept wondering, *Was this jet shot down by the commies? Were we under attack? Is this happening all over the country?* I hung around and tried to hear what the police were saying. Finally, I heard a policeman say that the pilot had radioed a distress call: the jet engine had failed.

All the adrenaline in me eventually faded, and I started to pedal slowly back to the farm. I had no idea what awaited me. As I put the bike in the garage, I heard Dad scream, *"Where the hell have you been?"* Mom came around the corner, and she was crying. Apparently, they had spent the last three hours searching for me. They didn't know about the plane crash. They didn't see the missing bike. They thought I had been in some sort of accident. Between sobs, Mom managed to get out, "We searched the canal, the silo, the bull pen. We searched everywhere. We were sure something terrible had happened to you." I tried to explain, but they kept saying things like, "You couldn't leave a note? Did you give any regard to how we'd feel when we got home and there was no sign of you?" I understood their feelings. I screwed up. I already knew what the punishment would be; they wouldn't talk to me for a month.

My interest in spies, communists, and mysteries continued; in fact, my interest actually increased. A rumor started to float around that the government was going to buy five thousand acres of farmland just to our south. Something about building a new airbase for long-distance bombers, the kind that could drop atomic bombs on Russia. This made Dad, Grandpa, and I real sad. The farmers that owned that land would lose something that they and their ancestors had worked on for generations. All their work, sweat, and tears would be gone. Sure, they were supposed to get fair market value, but there is really no way they could be compensated for their loss.

The news of the jet crash was the talk of Yorkville and all of Racine County. The local paper published the following:

BIGGEST BIT OF DEBRIS left when a jet fighter of the Air Force crashed Friday morning just east of Union Grove is this view of the tail section. The pilot was killed.

The crash happened shortly after 10 a. m. Friday on the Alvin Maurice farm when the jet plane, on a routine operational flight from O'Hare field, Chicago, developed engine trouble. Air Force investigators said the pilot had apparently tried to "ride it in" to a landing rather than bail out. The plane struck a slight rise in the plowed field and then roared up a slight incline, disintegrating as it went. The motor of the plane snapped off an oak tree 14 inches thick some 200 yards beyond the portion of the ship shown here. The body of the pilot lay about 100 feet beyond this point. Sheriff Walter Becker estimated that wreckage was scattered over a half mile area. Sheriff's deputies were assigned to guard the wreck scene until an investigation team from the Air Force could arrive to take over.

Photo by John Zwiebel

Photo thanks to John Zwiebel

JAMES R. VYVYAN SR.

CHAPTER TEN

A Learning Experience

THE PRETTIEST GIRL in school, Judy Springer, liked me. I had a hard time wrapping my head around that. Judy was blonde, with a shape like a young Marilyn Monroe, and blue eyes to boot. It was just too hard to believe that a girl like that would like a farm boy, plow boy, like me. For more than a year, I did nothing except perhaps say a few words to Judy, and then something happened that changed everything.

Bill Skewes and I were returning from the spring choral concert at Union Grove High School, when a 47 Chevy started to pass. I didn't think much about it until I noticed Judy in the passenger seat. The driver wasn't someone I knew, but it was pretty clear they were on a date. I decided I wasn't going to let them pass. I sped up to seventy, and they did too. I increased my speed to eighty, and they did too. I got up to eighty-five, and we were still neck and neck. Apparently, that was about top end for both cars, and we continued side by side. Common sense eventually prevailed on my part, and I slowed down and let them go by.

We traveled about two miles farther when I saw steam rising and cars pulling to the side of the road. The Chevy had T-boned an old Ford pickup, which was now tipped over and lying on the driver's side door. Bill and I pulled over and rushed to the accident. Of course, I looked for Judy first, and she was shaken and shivering. I wrapped my new leather jacket around her. The driver was semiconscious and muttering to himself. The big problem was the woman in the pickup. She was standing on the inside of the driver's door, and I could just see her head above the passenger side door. The gas tank was leaking badly, and I thought for sure it was going to explode. "Bill, we've got to help her!" The moment I said those words, it dawned on me that I was only doing this to impress Judy. (So we did the heroic thing, but at least on my part, it was for all the wrong reasons.) Between the two of us, we were able to pull the woman to safety. By that time, ambulances started to arrive, and they took all three people to the hospital.

That was how it started. It was only reasonable that I needed to go to Judy's house to retrieve my jacket. Judy was beyond grateful, and I got the idea that she really did like me. I did it; I asked her out for Saturday night. Now, I've had a few dates, and Judy has probably had a lot of dates, but we really hit it off. I don't think I've ever been with a girl that was so easy to talk to. We talked about school and our upcoming graduation. We talked about how there was really nothing to do in Union Grove. We talked about our parents, our friends, the upcoming summer vacation. We talked and talked and talked. I'd never known being with a girl could be so easy and so much fun. So that's how it started, and we became what you call an item. Soon we were going steady. She had my ring wrapped in Angora and wore it around her neck. I began to think she might be the one.

I'll never forget the night we decided to see the movie *From Here to Eternity*. Some of our friends had told us that it was a great movie. It was playing at the Westgate Outdoor Theater. I picked Judy up about eight, and she was looking fantastic. She had her hair in a ponytail, and she had on blue shorts with a white top. I might add that the white top had a bit of a low neckline. She was a real cupcake.

I had never taken a girl to an outdoor theater. I had heard all the stories about it being a passion pit and backseat bingo. I was somewhere between terribly excited and terribly scared. We started watching the movie, but then we started hugging and kissing. Somehow, my hand had a mind of its own as it worked its way closer and closer to Judy's breast. Finally, it arrived, and I thought I was going to explode. Just then a couple walked past our car and brushed the side; we both jumped.

I thought about that night all week. I wished I knew more about what was going on with me physically and mentally. The things I was doing and the things I wanted to do were scaring me. Many times Dad and Mom and I have driven by certain houses and one of them would say, "They had to get married, you know." It was like having to get married was a fate worse than death. I knew I didn't want that, but at the same time, I wanted more. I wanted more information, for one thing. Were my feelings normal? Was what we were doing bad? I didn't know where to go or what to do. Sure, some of my friends talked

JAMES R. VYVYAN SR.

a good game about what they had done, but I didn't know whether to believe them or not.

Later that week, as Dad and I were milking, I got very brave and said to Dad, "Dad, you've never told me about sex."

Dad took a moment before he replied. "You've been with cows."

How the hell do you respond to that? I hoped he wasn't implying that I had sex with cows. Was he saying that sex between a man and a woman was the same as sex with cows? Was he just so shocked by the question that he didn't know what to say? I felt more confused than ever.

Dad and Mom finally bought a TV. I'm sure they were close to the last people in Yorkville to buy a TV. Judy and I talked about it, and we noticed that the ten o'clock movie was going to be *It Happened One Night* with Claudette Colbert and Clark Gable. So we decided to spend Saturday night at my house. Dad and Mom stayed up until almost ten and then announced that it was their bedtime. Judy and I hugged and kissed a little as we watched the movie. Then it happened. I thought I heard something and looked in the direction of the door to my grandparents' side of the house and saw an eye watching us. Son of a bitch! Grandma was watching us! This was just too creepy. We gathered our things, and I took Judy home.

The next Friday night, we went to the Venetian Theater, but that's not what made the night memorable. On the way home, I thought about how we were interrupted at the outdoor theater and by my grandmother. Then my brain came up with a plan: at least I think it was my brain. The high school was adding on a new cafeteria, and I remembered a construction trailer on the back side of the addition. I drove right between the addition and the construction trailer. We wouldn't be visible to anyone.

I put my right hand around Judy, and we began to indulge in some long, slow, tender kisses. Soon, the kissing became far more passionate, and my left hand found its way to Judy's breast. That continued for several minutes, and then something totally unexpected happened. Judy's left hand grabbed my left hand, and I thought that meant I had gone too far. Unbeknownst to me, Judy had already unfastened her shorts, and she guided my hand down to a place I'd only dreamed of. It was so moist and so hot, and I felt a shudder go through Judy like she'd been struck by lightning. After a few minutes, I think we both knew that was as far as we could go. I started the car and let out the clutch. We didn't move, the wheels spun, and I could feel us sinking in the mud. Son of a bitch! I revved the engine—forward, back, forward, back—nothing. What the hell are we going to do?

Apparently, someone had heard the racket and called the cops. Before I knew it, Officer Vivian was at my door, "Whatcha doin', Johnny?" Of course, he knew exactly what we were doing, and I had a feeling the whole town would know soon. The tow truck came and pulled us out. What a night!

But it was a night the following weekend that topped it. Judy and I were planning to go to a birthday party for a friend of mine. Judy called about five and said she had a headache and couldn't go. I didn't think anything of it and just told her I hope she'd feel better soon. I went to Union Grove to get some gas, and at the station, I heard someone saying that the Rocky Marciano fight would be on the radio. I remembered that I had left my transistor radio at Judy's. I drove over and knocked on the door. Judy came to the door with her hair up in curlers; it was obvious she was going out. She said nothing, and I said nothing except, "I want my radio and my ring."

JAMES R. VYVYAN SR.

CHAPTER ELEVEN

McCarthy

GRANDPA HAS TOLD me about the Black Dog. I never really understood it until now. After all the great times Judy and I had, the fact that she would cheat on me and lie to me is devastating. I have difficulty forming any clear thoughts. It's like all my brain cells are firing at the same time. Part of me wishes I were dead so that I wouldn't feel this pain. Another part of me is numb and doesn't feel anything. Why would she do this? Why hadn't I been able to ask her what the hell is going on? Where do I go from here? In a few days, it will be graduation, and then what? What will it be like to go back to school and see Judy? Maybe she'll be walking down the halls with someone else; I couldn't stand that.

People have told me trouble comes in threes. As if I needed any more trouble, this morning I found my dog, Trooper, dead just like the other two. I can't even think about it. Dad investigated, but the result is the same—unknown, unsure. I just want to scream, shout, and swear!

Plus, for the last few weeks, Dad has been pushing me to make a decision about farming. Apparently, Grandpa has said he would transfer the farm to Dad if he knew that I would be there to carry on the family tradition. That's a lot of pressure for someone who hasn't even graduated from high school.

So for three days, I've lain on the couch watching TV. I told Mom and Dad I was sick. They don't know about Judy. They may think I'm sick about Trooper, and they would be partially right. Anyway, I've been watching TV for three days straight. I couldn't even tell you what I've been watching—everything and anything to take my mind off my problems. On the third day, Wisconsin senator Joe McCarthy came on the news. He said he could identify at least fifty-seven people in the government that were bona fide communists. Joe gave a persuasive speech, and this, together with the daily news about the communists taking over South Korea, hit a nerve. That's it!

I got Mom and Dad together and came right out with. "I'm going to join the army!"

They responded in unison, "You're what?"

"I'm going to join the army."

Mom asked, "Is it because of Trooper, or is there something else going on?"

"No, I just want to fight the commies and keep our country free."

Dad joined the conversation. "What about the farm? You know your grandpa is ready to sign over the farm if you commit to farming."

"I'm sorry, Dad, I can't make that commitment now. I promise, when I return in two years, I'll give you an answer."

Mom queried, "Have you thought about the possibility you could be killed?"

"Not really, I'm sure I'll be fine."

She followed up with, "What about your graduation? It's only a few days away."

"I can't say for sure if I'll be there or not."

Dad asked, "What's brought about this sudden change?"

"Well, I've been listening to Senator McCarthy, and he makes a lot of sense. He was a Wisconsin farm boy, so I trust him."

"Don't be too sure. I've heard some stories. One of them sticks in my mind. When he was going to Marquette University, he ran for class president. He and his opponent agreed to vote for each other. McCarthy won by one vote and admitted that he voted for himself. Don't be too sure about him."

"I trust him."

Now that I've announced it, I'm having second thoughts. Have I really thought this through? What if I did die? My next thought was, *It would serve Judy right. She'd be sorry then.* I thought about it some more. Number one, I just can't make a decision about farming now. It's too big and too important. Number two, I can't bring Trooper back to life, and there seems to be no way to solve the mystery. Three, I can't fix my relationship with Judy, but I'll bet she'll be sorry when she hears. Or will she?

JAMES R. VYVYAN SR.

CHAPTER TWELVE

My Son

M Y SON, JOHN, has thrown me for a loop. The idea of him fighting in Korea makes my blood run cold. It's also caused me to reflect not only on John but also my wife and myself.

I'm afraid I've let my wife and son down. Too many times I've let farmwork come before their needs and wishes. Once I overheard a friend say, "Tom works too hard to make any real money." I finally understand what he meant. I think back to the day that Ann begged me to leave this place and buy our own farm. Why did I turn her down? Why have I forced her to live in this house with my mother when my mother treats her like dirt? I think about all the times that John wanted to play and I brushed him off by saying "Sorry, got to work."

John has been nothing but a blessing, and I love him. He's worked so hard; he's done the work of a man since he was just a boy. So why am I unable to tell him these things? Why do I have such a hard time just having a conversation with him? Is it because he challenges me? In my head, I know that young men challenge their fathers from time to time. Young men, especially sons, have ideas of their own. Why haven't I given his ideas a fair chance? Could it be because my father has never really given my ideas a fair chance?

I'll never forget the day John asked me about sex and I responded with "You've been with cows." How could I be such a dolt? I have such a clear picture of that moment in my head. I can see just where he was standing, the position of his arms, and the look on his face. The question was such a shock; he and I have never talked about personal things. If I was half a man, I'd go to him today and have a real conversation about it, but I know I can't.

My gut wants to blame this situation on somebody or something. Maybe I could blame it on the Great Depression. When we were so close to losing our farm and I worked harder and longer than any person ever should. For two years, I really thought of nothing but work and how I was going to pay off the mortgage. Yes, I saved the farm, but something else was lost. Or maybe I could blame it on my mom. I've never really had a conversation with her. Maybe I don't know how because I was never taught or shown how to do it. Maybe because my parents' relationship was so strained, I haven't had any model to follow.

My head knows better. I've lived on this earth for nearly forty years. I've had plenty of time to grow beyond what my parents taught me. My parents lost a child, my brother; I can't blame them. No parent should have to go through the agony of losing a child. The truth is, I can't blame my shortcomings on anyone or anything but me. I love my son so much; if only I could tell him.

CHAPTER THIRTEEN

Korea

I CALLED SOME of the people I knew who had been in Korea. They pretty much agreed there was an advantage to being drafted over enlisting. The army expected more from the enlistees than they did from the draftees. Plus, they could easily tell who was who because the ID number for enlistees started out with RA (regular army) and the ID for draftees started out with US. In addition, a draftee was in for a two-year hitch, while the enlistee served three years. So I jumped in my car and headed for the draft office in Racine. The head of the draft board was a family friend, and I explained my situation.

He responded, "So you're volunteering to be drafted."

"Yes, sir!"

"Do your mom and dad know about this?"

"Yes, sir!"

"And you want to ship out ASAP even though you might miss your graduation."

"Yes, sir!"

"We can accommodate you, you'll be shipping out in three days."

So exactly one week from Judy's betrayal, I was on my way to Fort Leonard Wood, Missouri. I never did return to school or attend my high school graduation. As I boarded the DC3 at Midway Airport, I felt very much alone and very much afraid. I hadn't really prayed in a long time, but I prayed long and hard for God to keep me safe. I spent eight weeks of hell in basic training. Every terrible thing I had heard about basic was true and more. The next four weeks I spent at Fort Belvoir, Virginia. This was far better. I was treated better, worked less, and was trained in water supply. After training, I boarded a large troop transport ship along with three thousand other GIs. The stench from unwashed, vomiting, cigarette-smoking bodies was indescribable. Showers on board were salt water and left a body slimy. The head (latrine) was occupied by guys either vomiting or battling dysentery. The place to be was on deck, where the air was clear and on many days the sun shone brightly. We landed at the South Korean port of Inchon. My anxiety reached a new high when told the thunder-like rumbling was the sound of war with the front lines not far away. Most of these fears subsided when I was assigned duty in the Engineer Construction Battalion headquartered in Seoul.

Most buildings in Seoul had been destroyed by fighting; there was little public transportation, and water and electricity were scarce. Military installations provided for their own basic needs. Housing was primarily a ten-man-squad tent. The tent had a wooden floor and side walls. Our tent was cold in winter, sweltering in summer. We did derive some heat from a small oil-fired stove created from a gasoline barrel. In the winter, our breath would cause ice to form on the ceiling, and keeping warm was accomplished by purchasing a gook mattress and piling on as many blankets as possible.

Our job was to rebuild as many bridges and roads as we could. My role was to maintain a supply of material, such as concrete, tools, and water. A benefit to being in the supply function, we were able to barter surplus supplies such as gravel, flour, lumber, etc. Our French buddies wanted our flour for bread-baking, and we gladly liberated some of their wine rations. The wine came to them in bulk by tanker. We only had to provide a container, such as a five-gallon can.

There was seldom a shortage of beer and booze, and as you would expect, excess consumption was often the rule. Reverend Hollowell back in Yorkville would be shocked! I must have done something right because I eventually reached the rank of sergeant! As a sergeant, I received $140 per month, and I tried to save at least $100 every month.

In July of 1953, an armistice was signed, and the fighting ceased. I thought that might mean we could come home: I was mistaken. After the armistice, our unit was given the charge of building a Seoul headquarters for the Eighth Army. This was a major project, and we found ourselves building a library, gym, chapel, and lots of office space. A high priority was providing office space for Commanding General Maxwell Taylor. He was stern but an effective manager.

Months passed and I found myself experiencing my second Thanksgiving and Christmas away from home. Time passed and I felt

JAMES R. VYVYAN SR.

myself becoming a real man. I rejoiced when my orders were cut and my trip home commenced: train to Pusan; ship to Yokohama; ship to San Francisco; ferry to Camp Stoneman; plane to Midway Airport, Chicago; and bus to Fort Sheridan, Illinois, where I mustered out.

CHAPTER FOURTEEN

Homecoming

I'VE HAD A lot of time to think in the last two years. I've avoided coming home; Mom and I have exchanged letters, and there have been a few phone calls. Dad never wrote once. But I promised Dad when I left I would give him a decision about joining him on the farm. I've been weighing the pros and cons. For the pros, I listed: love tractors and farming is what I know. For the cons, I listed: uncertainty of the weather, milking 365 days a year, difficulty in finding more land, more land means bigger machinery—it's never ending, working with a dad who doesn't talk much, the Foxwell way of putting farmwork ahead of family, and danger. Danger is big. My uncle Joe died in a farming accident. Dad almost died when the tractor tipped over on him. I almost died when the bull attacked me. Thinking about it logically, there is no choice; I could never be a farmer.

I thought a lot about Judy. Finally, it dawned on me. I deserve better. I'm a good man, and I deserve a woman who will be honest and true. End of story. I also thought about Blackie and Trooper and decided I can't rest until the answer is known.

I mustered out at Fort Sheridan, took a bus to Milwaukee, and hitchhiked back to Yorkville and arrived unannounced.

It was a beautiful early June day, and Dad and Grandpa were in the yard working on the baler. When they saw me, they came running and yelling. Soon Mom, Dad, Grandpa, and Grandma were all shouting and hugging. It was swell.

Later that evening, after a wonderful home-cooked meal, I sat down with Mom and Dad. "Dad, I want to tell you about my decision."

"Before you do, I want you to know we've already made a deal with Grandma and Grandpa, the farm belongs to your mom and me."

"Thanks, that makes it a lot easier to tell you that my future won't be in farming."

"What are you going to do?"

"I don't know, but I do know that farming is not for me. I hope you're not too disappointed in me."

"I'm just glad you're home safe and sound."

"Dad, in the two years that I've been gone, have any other animals been killed?"

"No, thank God."

"Dad, I've got to know what killed the calf, Blackie, and Trooper."

"I'd love to know too, son."

The three of us talked on into the night as I tried to fill them in on Korea and the man I've become in the last two years. It was nearly midnight when Dad said, "I've got a cow that might be having a calf. I've got to go to the barn and check on her."

"Dad, let me, I know you're tired. It's the least I can do for you."

I walked slowly to the barn. It was a beautiful moonlit night, and the sweet smell of a well-run dairy farm was a treat, especially after the horrific smells of Korea. I turned on the barn lights, and I walked past the two horse stalls. I could see that Dad was taking the horse stalls out to make room for more cows. The next two pens were filled with baby calves that looked at me expectantly. Finally, I got to the one cow that was in the barn. She was contentedly chewing her cud, no calf tonight, and I turned to walk back to the house. It was then that I heard glass breaking, and in an instant, that end of the barn was ablaze. What the hell? The dry straw and the hundred-year-old wood were fully involved in an instant. I ran to open the side door so I could get the calves and the cow out. The door was blocked! It wouldn't move an inch. What the hell? I went to the far end door, same thing. There was only one other door, and I ran toward it. Meanwhile, the hundred-year-old barn wood was becoming an inferno. I reached the last door, and shit, it too was jammed, stuck, blocked somehow.

Now, I was worried not only about the animals but for myself too. What am I going to do? It dawned on me that there was a door in the haymow. I had nailed it shut two years ago, but I bet I could kick it open. I climbed the ladder to the haymow. Smoke was billowing up the opening as I climbed. The door was just to the left of the ladder in the haymow, and I gave it my best kick. Nothing! I kicked it again. Nothing! I gave it a third blow and it opened and I jumped out.

As I hit the ground, it knocked the wind out of me, and I lay there trying to catch my breath and clear the smoke from my lungs. Just as I was beginning to catch my breath, I heard, "I'm going to kill you, you fucker!" as someone jumped me. I could see the moonlight reflect off his knife as he brought it to my neck. "I'm going to kill you, you fucker!" and I thought I recognized the voice.

Before I could react, I heard, "That's enough!" and a second person launched himself at my attacker, and it felt like he hit him with a two-by-four. As soon as my attacker was off, I ran to the house, and I met Dad halfway there.

"Are you okay, John?"

"Call the fire department!"

"I already have."

"Call the police, I'm going to get a gun."

By now, the barn was totally involved in flames. There was no hope of saving the animals. Dad and I approached the fight scene, and I had the 12-gauge shotgun ready to fire. Luckily, the wind was blowing the flames and heat away from the scene. As we arrived, there were two men lying about six feet apart. The older man lay motionless with a knife sticking out of his chest. That man had a long gray beard, long matted hair, and raggedy clothes. The younger man was semiconscious, and I recognized him immediately.

CHAPTER FIFTEEN

Resolution

WE COULD HEAR sirens in the distance as they grew closer. I approached the dead man, and I couldn't believe it. "Dad, do you remember those Florsheim shoes I lost five years ago?"

"Sure do."

"This old guy is wearing them! I'm sure because of the funny doodads on each side of the shoes."

His shirt also looked vaguely familiar, but I couldn't quite place it. I turned my attention to the other man who was lying on the ground and bleeding profusely.

"Jon Gorzky! Why?"

"You ruined my life!"

"How the hell did I ruin your life?"

"You turned me in to the police for burning down that school."

"I did no such thing!"

"That day in the bathroom, you heard George and I talking about burning down the school."

"I did not hear what you said. I did not tell the police, and even if I did, you got what you had coming." No response. "Did you kill my dogs?"

"Yes."

Just then, Mom and Grandpa arrived on the scene. Mom took one look and ran to get a bandage for Jon's head. That's my mom! Grandpa took one look and simply said, "The Gorzkys have had it in for the Foxwells for generations, it's hard to understand."

The fire department arrived first. It was immediately clear that all they could do was to keep the nearby buildings from burning. Water was a problem even for that. Calls were made to Raymond, Dover, and Union Grove for additional tankers of water. Then Officer Vivian arrived and put the handcuffs on Jon Gorzky. I filled the officer in on what Jon had told me. Looks like Jon will be going away for a long, long time.

The officer, Dad, and I turned our attention to the dead man. Officer Vivian asked, "Do either of you recognize him?" We shook our heads.

"He's wearing a pair of shoes I lost five years ago. I recognized them because of the little doodads on the sides."

Dad offered, "Could he be the one that's been living in the old gravel pit?"

"Could be, but I'm shocked that he saved my life."

"I wonder why he was willing to risk his life to save you?"

"Could it be he's been watching us from afar for many years? Maybe he even thought of us as family."

"Dad, didn't you have a mysterious thing happen with some tiling a long time ago?"

"Yes, but I always thought it was my Uncle Ben or Uncle Walt that helped dig the trench. Now I'm not so sure. I'm also rethinking the fire that blackened the woodshed. Plus, we've had a number of small things missing. I always thought that we just misplaced them."

Officer Vivian checked him for identification. There was no wallet, but in his shirt pocket was an old faded picture. Written on the back in pen was "Mom-James-Sarah-Dad." Beneath the word James was written "me" in pencil. So whoever this guy was, his name was James. I owe James my life!

By now, the sun was peeking over the horizon. Other than the smoldering ruins of the barn, it could have been a beautiful day. I checked those blocked doors. Apparently, Jon had put three or four huge rocks against each one. It must have been quite a feat carrying them from the rock pile, which was over two hundred feet away. The cows started to make a racket. They didn't know any difference; they wanted to be milked just like every other day. Luckily, if there was any luck here, the Shafers had just sold their herd of cows. Tom Shafer felt he could make a better living at American Motors in Kenosha. With the help of the volunteer firemen, we drove the cows through the unplanted fields to the Shafers. Dad would continue milking the cows there until the barn was rebuilt.

So that was my homecoming. Oh, one more thing. I was honored to be part of the Iwo Jima float in the Racine Fourth of July Parade.

Apparently, the commander of the local American Legion post noticed that I had just completed my duty in Korea and gave me a call. The Iwo Jima float has four servicemen simulating raising the flag on Iwo Jima. I've seen that float in the parade for as long as I can remember. I felt it a real honor to be one of the four men raising that flag. Then a funny thing happened.

The parade route was about three miles long. Luckily, the weather was good, neither too hot nor too cold. I first noticed her at the Root River Bridge. One of the unfortunate things about the Racine Parade is the opening of the Root River Bridge. According to federal law, boats have the right-of-way, so if a boat wants to go up the Root River, the bridge tender has to open the bridge. The parade be damned. So we were waiting for the bridge to go back down. There was one unit in front of us, the Royal Airs. The Royal Airs were one of the nation's top drum and bugle corps. That's saying something because Racine is called the drum and bugle corps capital of the world. My eyes were drawn to one of the women tossing the rifles. She could toss that rifle a good twenty-five feet high, have it rotate five times, and catch it perfectly horizontal at waist height. Plus, she was as cute as any woman I'd ever seen. After the bridge returned to its position, I kept my eye on her for the next two miles. She never missed! As our units finished the parade, I sought her out and told her how fantastic she was. I thought I might have something here!

I spent the rest of the summer looking for a job. You'd think a young veteran fresh from Korea would be a good hire. Apparently, not many people felt that way. I asked myself, "What is it I really want to do?" The answer came to me that I wanted to work with tractors. I applied for a job at the Allis Chalmers Proving Grounds, and they hired me. They actually pay me to drive their biggest and best experimental tractors. Life is good!

EPILOGUE

I T'S THE BICENTENNIAL ceremony at the Yorkville Cemetery. I'm standing at attention as the honor guard is firing their salute to our country. As the firing subsides, my mind starts to wander. On my way here, I drove by the family farm. Houses are popping up like weeds in a bean field. Dad quit farming and subdivided the farm. Grandma and Grandpa still live in the old farmhouse. Mom and Dad built a beautiful, big house on the hill overlooking the farm. (They were careful to avoid the Indian mound.) Sure, it hurts to see that good farmland being turned into a subdivision, but I knew we'd made the right decision. Last Christmas, we had Mom and Dad over to our house, and at suppertime, Dad said, "Gee, I've never been able to stay for supper before, always had to milk the cows."

Mom added, "And it's a beautiful thing to go home to our own home."

It was then I truly knew that all was right with the world.

Oh, I mentioned our house. Remember that girl with the rifle? We married shortly after meeting, and she is the woman of my dreams. She is the woman that I deserve, and I trust her completely. Of course, she knows that she can trust me completely too. We have two wonderful children, James and Joe. Joe is named after my uncle who was killed in the silo accident. James is named after the man that saved my life.

I still work for Allis Chalmers. They have treated me royally. They encouraged me to go to school and get my engineering degree. I'm proud to say I did just that, and I've just finished testing the new Allis Chalmers 200 tractor. Plus, I still get to drive the biggest and best tractors Allis Chalmers makes. Life is complicated, but it can be wonderful too!

A BADGER TALE: ADVENTURES OF A WISCONSIN FARM FAMILY

TOM FOXWELL AND his family endure and, some would say, triumph over one hundred years of farming, romance, mystery, and adventure. *A Badger Tale* is a heartwarming saga of grandfather, son, and grandson and the trials and tribulations of growing up on a Wisconsin farm. The Foxwell family encounters the Great Depression, the Chicago World's Fair, World War II, rationing, the Cold War, Korea, and much, much more. This is a story of love, loss, death, and triumph that will hold you in its grasp until the very end.

CPSIA information can be obtained
at www.ICGtesting.com
Printed in the USA
FFOW04n1918010915
16479FF

9 781503 589032